I0621409

Olives in the Moonlight

Copyright © 2021 Snailfingers Publishing LLC All rights reserved.

This book or any portion thereof may not be reproduced or used in any manner whatsoever without the publisher's express written permission except for the use of brief quotations in a book review.

This is a work of fiction. Names, characters, places, and incidents either are the products of the author's imagination or are used fictitiously. Any resemblance to actual persons, living or dead, businesses, companies, events, or locales is entirely coincidental.

www.snailfingers.com

• Chapter One •

"Hello. I'm Jade, and I lost my father to cancer when I was ten years old."

"Yeah! fuck cancer," one of the kids shouted.

"That's good, Gene. You're getting your emotions out. Now let's try to express that in a more guided way," Jade responded. "So, this is monthly preliminary grief counseling for minors whose parents are terminally ill from cancer."

"In other words," Sienna interjected, "my wife is saying you all have something in common. Your parents have sent you here because they are sick, and they want you to start working through your grieving as early as possible. So, welcome to Colors of Grief therapy."

"Let's continue introductions. Why doesn't everyone say why they are here," Jade said. The room was silent for a moment.

Layla was seventeen and losing her mother to abdominal cancer. She had tried going to a couple of therapists, but she couldn't find the right fit. Her mother's colleague suggested the Colors program because it had recently been recognized for its non-profit work with youth.

"I think we are all here to be proactive. We need to prepare ourselves for the worst mentally-" Layla began.

"Sienna already said that," Dak interrupted.

"Since you are ready to talk, why are you here, Dak?" Sienna asked.

"Obviously, this doesn't apply to the rest of you, but I'm just here because I can't afford regular grief counseling," Dak responded.

"And to interrupt everyone else, apparently," Layla mumbled.

"What is that, Layla?" Sienna asked.

"I am here because I actually believe you can help me, not just because I don't have another choice. That's all."

"That's good. I'm glad you feel that way. Anyone else want to share why they are here?"

"Well, I think although we are here for grief counseling, maybe we could also support each-" Another person in the group began.

"Excuse me," Dak interrupted. "I'm sorry, Layla, but someone else could be sitting in that seat. I mean, like someone who 'doesn't have another choice' or whatever."

because it had recently been recognized for its non-profit work with youth.

"I think we are all here to be proactive. We need to prepare ourselves for the worst mentally-" Layla began.

"Sienna already said that," Dak interrupted.

"Since you are ready to talk, why are you here, Dak?" Sienna asked.

"Obviously, this doesn't apply to the rest of you, but I'm just here because I can't afford regular grief counseling," Dak responded.

"And to interrupt everyone else, apparently," Layla mumbled.

"What is that, Layla?" Sienna asked.

"I am here because I actually believe you can help me, not just because I don't have another choice. That's all."

"That's good. I'm glad you feel that way. Anyone else want to share why they are here?"

"Well, I think although we are here for grief counseling, maybe we could also support each-" Another person in the group began.

"Excuse me," Dak interrupted. "I'm sorry, Layla, but someone else could be sitting in that seat. I mean, like someone who 'doesn't have another choice' or whatever."

• Chapter One •

"Hello. I'm Jade, and I lost my father to cancer when I was ten years old."

"Yeah! fuck cancer," one of the kids shouted.

"That's good, Gene. You're getting your emotions out. Now let's try to express that in a more guided way," Jade responded. "So, this is monthly preliminary grief counseling for minors whose parents are terminally ill from cancer."

"In other words," Sienna interjected, "my wife is saying you all have something in common. Your parents have sent you here because they are sick, and they want you to start working through your grieving as early as possible. So, welcome to Colors of Grief therapy."

"Let's continue introductions. Why doesn't everyone say why they are here," Jade said. The room was silent for a moment.

Layla was seventeen and losing her mother to abdominal cancer. She had tried going to a couple of therapists, but she couldn't find the right fit. Her mother's colleague suggested the Colors program

"What's your problem, dude?" Layla responded.

"I heard you mumbling under your breath," Dak said.

"Well…" the girl sitting across from Dak looked around before speaking, "I have tried other forms of counseling at different price points, but I just thought I would try something new. I figured if you're volunteering, you must really care."

"Again, someone who doesn't have the option to try out 'other price points' could be in your seat too," Dak said. "I just thought this therapy was for people like me- people who actually can't afford help."

"I need help too. My mother is dying…" Layla said, looking at the floor.

"I mean, he has a point. The majority of us are-" someone butted in.

"Enough. This isn't why we're here," Jade interjected.

"This is bullshit." Layla was getting irritated.

"This is not about anyone's financial background or upbringing. Money isn't going to save anyone's parent, and not having money doesn't mean that your parent won't survive," Sienna encouraged.

"Sienna and I came from different backgrounds, and both of us lost a parent when we were too young to understand how to cope. That is why we are here to help you," Jade said, "Now, can we please finish introductions."

The introductions did not continue smoothly, so Sienna removed Dak and Layla from the group. She took them to a separate room to discuss their behavior. It was clear that their issues were beyond grief counseling, and they needed some additional assistance.

"This disruption is intolerable. For these meetings to be effective for everyone, we all need to work together and support each other."

"I am sorry," Layla responded, "but I feel like I was being singled out. I don't know if this is the right place for me."

"Why is that?" Sienna asked.

"Well, maybe he is right. Maybe I should just try to figure things out on my own," Layla said.

"We are here to help each other," Sienna responded.

"I wasn't trying to be rude. It's just that- never mind. I guess I just feel like I have nowhere else to turn. Maybe we both belong here," Dak said.

Sienna talked with them until the end of the session. It seemed to her that they were dealing with something more than just first-day jitters. Once the session ended, Jade joined the conversation.

"What happened today is unacceptable," Jade spoke sternly. Dak and Layla could see that she was upset. Jade breathed in deeply and let it out through her nostrils. "I think it would be best if the two of you left the group, but it seems like Sienna has already taken the initiative in this situation."

"I think that if I can work with the two of them in a separate session, it would allow them to work through their differences. Then maybe we could move forward a bit more amicably in the group," Sienna offered.

"So, you want the two of us to have a separate session together, away from the group?" Layla asked.

"Exactly! Essentially you'll have a couple of sessions with me while still attending group therapy. Of course, I would love to see you both individually, but a dual session is the only thing I can offer for the sake of time and budgeting. Regardless, it will be beneficial for the two of you. It is, however, your decision." Sienna looked at Jade, and Jade nodded her head. Layla and Dak reluctantly agreed.

"I don't mean to be rude again, but the session already ran a little bit over time, and if I don't leave right now, I'm going to miss my bus," Dak pressed.

"Perfect," Sienna said. "Layla, why don't you give Dak a ride home since it was your conversation that pushed back the end of our session. Maybe you can get to know each other."

"Ugh. How far do you live?" Layla rolled her eyes.

"In a car? Only fifteen minutes," Dak responded.

"Fine. Let's go."

The car ride was quiet. There was only an occasional "make a left here" from Dak. To his surprise, Dak was comfortable for once; he was a shy kid, an introvert by nature. Riding the bus everywhere meant being around strangers all the time. Though Layla was a stranger, it was nice to share his commute with only one other person.

Layla was thinking the exact opposite: she was mad that she was driving home the kid that gave her such a hard time during therapy. However, she would never refuse to help someone less fortunate. Also, giving Dak a ride home would prove that he was wrong about her.

Layla started to notice the environment changing drastically. South Tarino wasn't anything like North Tarino. She had always known that this wasn't a good part of town but hearing about it differed from experiencing it in person. Some fences needed to be fixed, and there were so many broken down cars. The yards that did have grass needed to be cut, and it was slightly louder here. Layla parked her car on the curb outside of Dak's home.

"You don't have to say it," Dak broke the ice.

"Say what?"

"Things got a little out of hand during therapy, and I was an asshole. I just want to apologize and thank you for the ride home."

Layla was in complete shock. This was not the boy whom she had met just an hour ago. He seemed gentle and humble.

"We both kind of played our part in the entire thing. It's fine," Layla shrugged and smiled.

Dak thanked her once again for the ride home and began to walk toward his house. An old car drove by blasting music, and suddenly Layla was reminded of where she was. Like herself, Dak was losing a parent, but with significantly fewer resources to cope with it.

Layla called out to Dak, "Hey, if you ever need a ride from therapy or anything like that, just ask."

"Well, I do need a ride somewhere. Let me run inside to grab my bags, though. You can come in if you'd like."

He turned to walk away but stopped. "Wait. Were you asking me that seriously? I feel like I sort of jumped the gun."

"It's fine. Where exactly do you need to go?"

"Thanks. I just need to go to the grocery store." It was perfect timing. Carrying a couple of pounds of groceries on the bus was always embarrassing and drew too much attention to Dak.

Layla walked into the brown home. She was immediately met with the stench of old cigarettes, carpet, and sheet vinyl flooring that had been installed many years ago. What was once a living room looked as if it had become someone's workstation.

"Is this all your stuff?" Layla asked.

"Yeah. I've kind of just been living here. I mean, since my dad has been in the hospital, there is no one else in the house anyway."

"What do you mean? Where's your mom?"

"She died a while ago."

"Oh. So, your dad is a single parent?"

Dak nodded. "yep."

"My mom is all I've got left too. My dad ran off when I was a little kid, so I never really knew him." Layla looked around. She walked over to a table and saw something that stood out. There was a pile of papers that had been written on with an actual typewriter. She felt like it was daring her to read it.

"What's this about," she asked as she picked it up.

"Um, just- it's about a girl and some turtles. My mom wrote it."

Layla began to read it and was immediately drawn in. "This is really good. What else happens?"

"Well, the girl is studying marine biology, and she really likes turtles."

"It seems like more than that." Layla shuffled through the papers.

"She volunteers at a sea life conservation and finds a batch of Olive Ridley sea turtles on the beach, so she has to protect them until they hatch."

"Wow, I like that. My mom is- or was, I guess- editor in chief at a pretty big publishing company. She always brought books home for me when I was younger. I loved the illustrations, and I've been an artist ever since."

"Thanks. My mom never got to finish it, so I started to finish her story. I don't really know if I'll be able to finish it, but I might eventually." They were silent for a moment. "Anyways, we should go before it gets too late."

• Chapter Two •

Dak hadn't thought much about Layla since their last session, but as she drove them to their first private session with Sienna, he became more grateful for her assistance. Once they were parked, Dak thanked Layla for the ride.

"I thought it would be awkward to say this before," she responded, "but so far, I am kind of glad that Sienna made me give you a ride. It makes going into this therapy thing a little less intimidating if I can go with someone else," Layla responded.

"Yeah, but I was kind of mad because I am so poor that I have to share a therapist," Dak said.

"I thought the opposite. I was excited that I would be able to find more people like me."

"Well, then I'm glad Sienna stuck us together too."

Sienna was right. Once they started to get to know each other, they were more comfortable together, so it was easier for them to open up during the session.

"I think sometimes I get overwhelmed by small things just because I am afraid of losing my dad. Like this weekend, for example, I won't be able to watch Halloween movies with him like I'm used to. I guess I feel like I wouldn't have to worry so much about him if we had more money because then he could get the best care. We don't even have the money for transportation, so I wouldn't be able to get to my dad in an emergency," Dak vented.

"Does it make you worry that you don't have anyone else to fall back on or that you don't have another parent to help you through this?" Sienna asked painfully.

"Are you alright," Layla asked Sienna.

"I'm fine. It's just a little pregnancy cramp."

"When is the baby due," Dak asked.

"Early next year," Sienna smiled while placing her hand on her bulging stomach. "But back to you, Dak."

"Sorry, Yeah. At least I had my dad when my mom passed. Now I basically have to support myself, so this time it's much harder."

"How was it when you lost your mom?" Sienna asked.

"Is it okay if I don't answer that?"

"Not if you don't want to. And what about you, Layla? If you lose your mom, you don't have another parent to help you either."

"Well, I've never lost a parent before. My dad was never really around to begin with, so I don't know what it is like to lose someone. I think I kinda feel overwhelmed too," she paused for a minute. "Can I just bring up something positive instead?"

"Yes. Maybe discussing something positive will help both of you clear your minds," Sienna said.

"After our last session, you told Dak and me to get to know each other. When I dropped him off at home that night, he showed me a story that he was working on. I think it's really good. I wanted to bring it up and encourage him to finish it."

"That's really nice, Layla. What do you think, Dak?"

"I don't know. I haven't gotten around to finishing it. Maybe I will someday."

"Why do you seem reluctant?" Sienna asked.

"I just don't know if it is something that I can accomplish," Dak said. "It's my mom's story, so I'm scared. She worked hard on it, and I don't want to mess it up."

"Do you feel like this is a task that she left behind for you to complete? Do you feel obligated to finish it?"

"I feel like it needs to be finished because that's what she wanted, but I don't want to disappoint her."

"Well, Dak, maybe that is something that we should discuss further. I don't want either of you to take away from each other's time, so if there is anything you would like to add, Layla, feel free to do so. If not, it is fine for you to continue if you would like, Dak."

Dak was ready to move on from the topic of the book, so Layla took the opportunity to talk about her mother. Sienna ended the discussion by prompting Dak to consider writing a letter to his mom. If he could process some emotions about his mother's book, then perhaps he could finish writing it.

When the session ended, Dak and Layla sat in her car for a moment.

"Did you really mean what you said today," Dak asked, "about the book, I mean?"

"Definitely. The little that I did read was great, and I think what you added to the story was fantastic. You're a good writer, just like your mom." Layla smiled.

"Thanks. No one has read the entire thing, so I don't know if it is any good. I mean, I like what my mom wrote, but no one's read my writing before."

"Doesn't your dad like it?"

"I didn't start writing it until after my dad got sick, and I haven't had the courage to show it to him yet."

"I bet he would love to see you finish it. You know, if you do decide to finish it, I could even do the cover design for you and help edit it."

Layla grabbed her backpack from the back seat of her car and pulled out her sketchbook.

"I already started making some sketches of what I pictured the cover to look like based on what I've read so far."

"I can't believe you did that. That actually gives me a little bit of motivation," Dak said as he flipped through the pages.

"That's great! You can keep the one you like on your table for more motivation."

"Thanks. I feel like you really do care about this."

"It's just exciting to meet someone else who is into books the way I am. I don't really have any friends, and my boyfriend doesn't really relate to me in that way. Not that he's a bad guy or anything, it's just that he's more into movies than books."

"I mean, he sounds cool."

"Yeah, but I'm not really interested in the kind of movies he likes, so that's why I'm glad that I have someone to be creative with."

"He doesn't mind you driving me to therapy, though, right? I mean, I don't want him to get the wrong idea."

"Um," Layla hesitated, "I don't really know. I haven't brought it up to him. It's not like it matters. I'm just helping you out."

"Alright. Well, I am glad you feel that way about finding someone to be creative with."

On the way home, Dak and Layla talked more about the books they had read, and they realized they both liked dramas. Discussing their favorite authors and scenes in books gave Dak a sense of assurance about his own writing because he knew at least Layla would like it.

• Chapter Three •

A month had passed since the last therapy session, and Dak and Layla had become much closer. Layla gave Dak a ride home from therapy and decided to hang out for a bit. Dak had not mentioned it before, but he was very self-conscious about the house.

"Sorry for the smell. My dad and I don't smoke. We inherited the carpets, and that's the smell they came with," he said.

He explained to Layla that his father had used the little money they got from his mother's life insurance to buy the home. It was abandoned and in dire need of maintenance, but they were homeless, and that was their way out. His father's plan was to do the minor repairs himself while saving money to contract out the rest of the rehab. Unfortunately, things changed once he got sick.

"I could never imagine being without a home, and I don't really care about the smell of your carpets," Layla responded.

At that moment, a weight had been lifted off of Dak's shoulders. He was so worried about Layla judging him that he didn't even consider that she might not even care. Layla joked about how he should just rip out the carpet and worry about replacing the flooring later.

Dak asked Layla to take a seat while he started cooking. "Maybe the food will make it smell better in here," he thought. Layla had been doing her homework at the kitchen counter, but she was getting distracted by Dak's cooking because she wasn't used to home-cooked meals. She never paid attention to how her mother prepared food, and half of the time, they ate at restaurants anyway.

"I am still very impressed that you cook for yourself," Layla chimed in.

"I actually don't cook that often, but I am making some of my dad's favorite dishes for Thanksgiving. I want to surprise him tomorrow with some real home-cooked food."

"That's very thoughtful of you. I think you're a pretty good son."

"It's not much, but maybe it will lift his spirits, you know?" Dak said as he pulled out the aluminum baking dish from the oven. "And I think my stuffing has turned out quite nice. Here, try some."

"If this is nasty, I'm going to be so mad," Layla said as she grabbed the spoon and dipped it into the tray.

"Just eat it."

Layla took a bite and began to stutter, "yis is yewy hawt."

Dak laughed. "Why didn't you blow on that before eating it?"

The food in her mouth eventually cooled down, and she was able to taste the flavor of Dak's cooking. It was delicious. She hadn't had stuffing this good in years.

"This is actually pretty good. I'll give you one thousand credits for it."

"What? Credits? What are you talking about?"

"I'm sorry, I don't know why I said that. It's just this thing I always do with my mom."

"It's fine. What is it exactly?"

Layla's stomach jumped as she explained the tradition. She and her mother had always given actions an arbitrary number whenever they wanted to give each other a compliment. She told him how she hadn't done that in months since her mother was sick. Dak thought it was a great idea. He told her it was absurd that she hadn't given him one million credits.

"I was just thinking about my mom, and I guess it was a Freudian Slip."

"Floridian slip?"

"No. Freud. Like, Sigmund Freud?"

"I don't understand what he has to do with your mom."

"A Freudian Slip is when you are subconsciously thinking of something, and you accidentally say it. Anyway, please don't tell anyone about the credits. It's kind of embarrassing."

"I have no one to tell."

"Good. So, what are you making for your dad?"

"Well, you just tasted my bomb stuffing, and I am going to attempt a sweet potato pie and some mashed potatoes."

"Mashed potatoes are my mom's favorite."

"We can make her some mashed potatoes and take her some stuffing too."

"I don't know, won't it hold you up," Layla asked.

"No, I'm not visiting my dad until tomorrow. I can cook his food later tonight. I don't sleep that much anyhow."

"Well, I never cook, so I don't know if I will be of much help."

"It's just mashing potatoes, plus I already made the stuffing," Dak said with a smile.

They started to cook, and as she had promised, Layla was a wreck in the kitchen. But, Dak didn't give up on her. He showed her how to peel potatoes and how to cut them into smaller bits before boiling. Layla had gotten comfortable, and for a minute, she had forgotten her mother was in the hospital dying. She hadn't had this much fun in a while. This was the first time Dak had any guest over. He had gone to therapy for support and, in return, had found a friend and so much more.

As they poured the water into the potatoes to boil, Dak asked, "hey, this is a silly question, but are you into music, like, records?"

"Well, that depends. What do you have?"

"I got a test for you."

"Never heard that one," Layla said with a smirk.

"Pshh, you know what I mean," Dak grinned as he walked to the record player. He glanced over his shoulder at Layla as if she couldn't see him looking at her. "I got something," he said as he pulled the record out of the sleeve.

The music began to play. Dak's eyes met back up with Layla's, and he saw a tiny smile on her face. It was the look a chess master had before yelling, "checkmate." The music slowly started to blend with the song's vocals. Dak watched as the lyrics leaving Layla's mouth perfectly aligned with the vocalist on the record.

"I can't believe you know this song." Dak was mesmerized.

Layla just kept singing while slowly bobbing her head.

"Ok, you passed the test. One million credits."

Layla laughed and began shrugging her shoulders up and down while pointing toward the ceiling.

"Two million credits, and that's my final offer."

"I'll take it," she said with a smile.

They began to talk about music, discussing all of the records that Dak had. He was surprised to learn that she had owned many of the same recordings as he had. Layla was impressed. She didn't know anyone her age that listened to as many old bands and soloists as she had. They joked about how all of their favorite acts were either dead or too old to tour. Layla mentioned how cool it would be to see video performances of some of her favorite songs.

Layla was a beautiful girl, and she let off a certain kind of confidence. It didn't help that she was well off, and Dak was living in poverty. Usually, when they talked to each other, Dak would mostly speak to the ground. Layla had noticed this about him early on, but she had never thought much of it. They had gotten really deep into their conversation when Dak suddenly realized they had been making eye contact the entire time. The room got quiet, and Dak bolted to the kitchen.

"Those potatoes should be done already," he said.

Once the potatoes were done boiling, Dak showed her how to mash them. They cleaned up the kitchen, wrapped up Layla's mother's food, and headed to Torino General Hospital.

When they arrived, Dak told Layla that he would wait outside of the room to allow her some space with her mom, but Layla insisted that he meet her.

"Hey, lady! Who is your friend?" Layla's mom said with the little energy she had.

"This is my friend, Dak. We met at grief counseling."

Dak was too nervous to speak. Layla's mother was like a wilted flower. Even though she was sick, you could still see that she was a beautiful woman. Her skin was copper, like Layla's. She also had freckles posted on opposite sides of her face. She radiated the same kind of confidence as her daughter.

"Hi. I'm, uh, Dak," he said nervously.

Her mother replied, "Aw, he's so shy and cute. I like him, Layla."

"I made you something real to eat for Thanksgiving, so you don't have to eat that hospital food," Layla said as she handed her mother the plate. Her mother bit into the stuffing and mash potatoes.

"Nope," she said, shaking her head, "my daughter didn't make this. It's too good. She can't even boil water."

Dak and Layla looked at each other and laughed.

"So, I might have had some help, but the love you taste is all me," Layla admitted with a smile.

Layla's mother thanked Dak for teaching her daughter to cook, but he downplayed his part in it. He even told her it was all Layla's idea. She seemed really happy when she was with her mother. This was her moment, and he didn't want to spoil it. Layla and her mother talked for an hour, occasionally bringing him into the mix.

"Oh, Dak, I wish you could have met me when I was a year younger and more lively," her mother said.

Everything was going well until the doctor walked in and asked if Layla and Dak could step outside for a moment. As they waited outside, Dak sat down while Layla paced the floor.

"Usually, when the doctor asks to talk to the patient alone, it means something is wrong," Layla said. She wouldn't stop pacing. Layla just kept going on about how worried she was. Layla was so anxious she started to cry as she rambled.

Dak reached out his arm and grabbed her by the hand. She stopped pacing.

"It's going to be okay. Remember what we talked about in therapy. You can get through this. We will get through all of this shit," Dak said. Layla nodded her head in agreement while giving him a hug. Soon the doctor came out of the room.

"Hey, is everything alright with my mom," Layla asked.

The doctor told her it would be best to speak with her mother on the matter. Layla rushed back into the room. Her mother informed her that she was given four months to live, and she wanted to go through with a living funeral. Layla was devastated. She cried and talked to her mother for another fifteen minutes before leaving abruptly. Dak was in the hallway when he saw Layla storm out of the room.

The car ride home was quiet.

"I feel so bad. I just wanted to do something nice for your mom. I didn't think our visit would turn out like this," Dak started to apologize.

"Dak, you didn't make my mother ill. I was going to get that news regardless. Bad news aside, I really enjoyed myself tonight. It was sweet how you cooked for my mom."

Eventually, the conversation shifted, and Layla dropped Dak off home. She stopped him before he got out of the car.

"Hey, thanks for tonight with my mom and all. I really appreciated it," Layla said.

"It's nothing." He turned around and started walking toward his front door.

"One million credits," Layla said as she drove away.

Dak smiled and continued walking toward the house.

• Chapter Four •

The park was Layla's happy place. She had always gone there as a child with her mother. It was quiet and filled with subjects to sketch. It was the perfect day to go as it was a beautiful Saturday afternoon. Layla had made plans weeks ago to go with Mitchell, and she made sure her schedule was clear for their date. As time went on, Layla grew frustrated because she had not yet heard from Mitchell, so eventually, she texted him. Mitchell read her text and immediately called.

"Hey, babe. I know we are supposed to go to the park today, but some of the college guys invited a couple of Honor Society seniors to play golf and-"

"So, you are calling me to cancel our date to go and play golf with your friends," Layla snarled.

"No. These guys aren't my friends. I'm just trying to network, and they can open doors for my future."

"I'm really upset about my mom right now. I thought we could talk about it and take a walk."

"Well, she's in the hospital, which is the best place for her to be right now. We can talk about it tonight when I get back from golfing."

Mitchell was a brilliant student with a bright future ahead. Layla hoped that she would have a special place in his life, even if she couldn't picture how just yet.

She sighed. "It's okay, go play golf. We can hang out next week or something-" there was a knock on her door. "Wait, hold on."

"One eight hundred flowers, ma'am, can you sign?"

Mitchell had already sent her apology flowers. She assumed that he had sent them hours ago, already knowing he would cancel the date. Layla signed for the gift and thanked Mitchell for the flowers. Just like that, she had been stood up, and Mitchell was on his way to play golf. Layla didn't really care about the flowers. She was disappointed in herself for withholding her emotions about Mitchell canceling the date. As she sifted through her thoughts, her phone began to buzz. It was Dak. She answered the phone like a shipwrecked sailor flagging down a passing boat.

"Hey!" She relaxed her voice. "I mean, what's up?"

"I think I finished my mom's book." Dak sounded both surprised and nervous. "Do you think you could read it and tell me if it's any good?

"I can actually come over right now and work on it with you. I was kinda on my way out of the door anyways."

Once Layla got to Dak's, she could see that he had spent the last couple of days writing. He looked dehydrated, and the skin below his eyes was darker than usual.

"Here." Layla handed Mitchell's flowers to Dak as a "congratulations on finishing your story" joke.

"You brought flowers?"

"Mitchell bought you flowers," Layla joked with a smile.

"You keep them. I don't want to get involved," Dak said nervously as he attempted to hand the flowers back.

"Relax. It was a joke, silly." Layla peeked her head around to look behind Dak, and the living room was a tad bit messy. "Do you always write in the living room?"

"I don't really have anywhere else to write. I only leave my house to visit my dad, go to therapy, and get food."

"I think I have somewhere better for us to work today. You need to get outside," Layla said.

Dak was always comfortable writing alone. Just asking Layla to help him edit the story was a big step for him. He was hesitant, but he thought maybe it was for the better. As much as he liked being to himself, he also enjoyed Layla's company. Dak agreed to go, and Layla drove them both to her favorite park.

The park was beautiful. The sun was grazing the tiny hairs on his arms as he waited for Layla to lock up the car. They found a spot near a mixed patch of plants, some wilting, and some full of life. When they sat on the bench, he turned to hand her his draft, but he stopped mid-motion.

"Hey, there's something I need to say before you read this," Dak said.

"What is it?"

"My writing might not be any good because I'm dyslexic."

"I don't think that should make a difference, all writing needs editing, or else my mother would have been out of work a long time ago. I'm sure your writing is fine."

Dak felt relieved. He allowed Layla into a sacred place. As Layla read the story, she didn't say anything. The silence was intoxicating. Dak didn't know what to say.

"Is it really that bad?" he asked.

"What?" Layla responded. "No, it's fine. I'm just really trying to get a grasp on what is going on in the story." Layla looked at his face, and she could see that Dak was nervous about her reading his work in front of him. She thought maybe they could take a break from it. She stopped reading and said, "you know what, I think in time we will be more comfortable working together, but for now, we can talk about other stuff if you want."

"You sure? I mean, I don't want to take up too much of your time."

"It's fine. I can read the rest of this when I get home. I actually want to edit this as fast as possible because I think you should enter your story into the Gold Pen Scholarship."

"Gold Pen? What's that?"

"It's a scholarship program that will give you a writing grant as long as you register for college after graduating. I mean, you do plan on going to college, right?"

Dak told her how he just figured he would go to community college because of his financial situation. He didn't even think his writing was good enough for reading, let alone a scholarship. But Layla said she was confident that he could do it. Dak was afraid of rejection and didn't think he was ready to submit his writing.

"I know you don't think you can do it, and you might not believe me when I say this, but your writing is pretty unique, and I believe in you."

"I guess I can try."

The two decided to explore the park for a while. Layla explained to Dak that she had been longing to go to this park lately because she hadn't been in a while. She told him she had always gone with her mother. There were great memories there, and Layla just wanted to be reminded of the good times. He asked her why she had waited so long to come, and she told him how Mitchell was supposed to take her, but he changed plans last minute.

"You know, you could have just come by yourself. I don't think you should let anyone keep you from doing what you want to do." Dak paused, "Wait. I'm sorry, I didn't mean to say it like that."

"No, you're right in a way," she sighed. "You are so independent, Dak, and I'm not. It's so hard for me to be by myself. I think that's what I fear the most about my mother being sick. If she passes away, I don't know how to be on my own."

"The truth is I'm scared as well. I'm actually pretty fucking terrified of losing my dad."

Layla began to cry, "This is so fucked up. Here the two of us are, on a beautiful day, and our parents are dying. I thought coming here would make me feel better, but I just feel worse."

Dak felt terrible, he was upset about his father's sickness, but he had been able to keep it together. Layla was having an emotional moment, and he felt like he needed to make her feel better somehow.

"Hey, what's the best part of this park that you remember?"

"I don't know the swings, I guess."

"I think you need to cry and let it all out, but why not do it while swinging?"

"Fuck it." Layla bolted toward the swings.

"That's not fair! You got a head start." As he caught up to her and approached the swings, she was already basking in victory. "You cheated, but you still won," he said. Dak quickly ran behind her and pulled the swing chain back. He pushed her on the swing until she forgot about their conversation.

"Ahh," Layla yelled in happiness. "I'm on top of the world!" Layla asked him if his arms were tired, but Dak enjoyed pushing her on the swing. She seemed so happy in this moment, and he wanted her to savor it for as long as his arms would allow her to.

"So tell me more about you and your mom. Have you two talked about you know…"

"Yeah, there is this eulogy I have to give at my mother's living wake."

"People actually have those?"

"Well, my mother wants to make her peace and say goodbye to everyone while she still can. But, that's the problem: I don't know how to say goodbye," Layla said.

Dak continued to push her on the swing. The wind was blowing, and her perfume was creating a scented breeze with every push. Dak suggested that maybe she didn't have to say goodbye in the eulogy. She and her mother had come to this park and played on these swings many times, and he thought it would be special if she could capture those moments in words. He stopped pushing her and walked over to his backpack. Layla stuck out her feet and planted them into the sand. As Layla walked back to the bench, Dak pulled out a notebook from his bag.

"I've got an idea," he said.

"Ok."

"I'm going to interview you about your mom so you can use the transcript as an outline for your eulogy," he said. Layla wasn't sure if his idea would work, but she didn't have any ideas of her own, and she really needed to start working on writing.

The first question was about Layla's best memory with her mother. Layla described her best memory with her mom, but that wasn't her favorite memory. Layla told Dak that her favorite memory with her mom was the day before her ninth birthday. Her mother had decided to surprise her and signed her out of school early. Then, they went to a fancy restaurant and rented movies to watch together.

"Why do you think she did it the day before?" Dak asked.

"Well, it was the start of my birthday week."

"Wait, a birthday week? Don't tell me you're one of those birthday divas that need an entire week of celebrations."

"Yes, all seven days unless there is a holiday, you know," Layla snorted as she laughed. She covered her nose in embarrassment.

"What was that?" Dak laughed.

"I don't know why I just snorted like a pig. Well, I guess I do that sometimes when I'm laughing. It's so lame."

Dak started to snort like a pig, "I-THINK-IT'S-CUTE."

"No, please stop!" she laughed. The two continued on with the interview.

"Okay, last question. What is one word that you would use to describe your mom?"

"That's a pretty hard one." Layla thought for a few minutes. "I don't know. I will have to get back to you on that one."

They talked about everything and ended up staying at the park much longer than they had intended. Before they left, Dak picked up a leaf from the ground and gave it to Layla. He told her to take it to her mother so she could have a piece of the park with her in the hospital room.

• Chapter Five •

Dak and Layla sat in his living room, which he cleaned out to give them space to write. Dak put his mom's typewriter on the coffee table and sat cross-legged on a pillow on the floor. The surface was littered with papers and Layla's art supplies. She preferred to work on her laptop if she helped Dak write, so she pulled up an old side table and sat in Dak's dad's comfy chair. If she didn't have anything to do for him, she still brought her homework, and they kept each other company.

They were making progress on the book when Dak noticed the time.

"I usually go to visit my dad around this time, so maybe we should finish this later," Dak said.

"We could go together. I can drive you," Layla said.

"I don't think my dad would mind, but-"

"You met my mom. I'd be excited to see your dad," she insisted.

"Alright, just don't mention anything about the living room. I haven't told him."

"Okay, okay. Let's go."

They left their stuff where it was and walked outside to get into the car.

"Hey, Layla, you left your lights on," Dak noticed.

"Oh, crap." Layla tried to turn on the car, but it stalled. She turned the key again and again for two minutes before giving up. She waited then tried once more. Nothing. She called her insurance company to tow her car, and she and Dak talked outside while they waited. It was an hour and a half before her car was towed, and the sun was going to set soon.

"I'm sorry we won't be able to visit your dad," Layla said.

Dak shrugged. "It's alright. We can take the bus."

"I've never taken the bus before, and it's going to get dark soon. Is that safe?"

"Sure. I do it all the time."

"How do you buy a ticket?"

"You mean a bus pass?" Dak laughed. "I have one in my wallet. It's good for the whole month. Do you have any cash?"

"No. I really only use my card."

"That's fine." Dak checked his wallet, "I'll buy you a day pass once we get on." They walked to the bus stop together, and Dak thanked Layla for helping out with the book. "I know my mom would have really appreciated it," he said.

"I have always wanted to work on a book, but I have never had the courage to actually do it," Layla said. "So, how do we know when the bus is going to come?"

"Let me check my phone. I should have done this before we left, but a new one comes every fifteen minutes, so if we missed the last one, we wouldn't have to wait long."

As Dak pulled out his phone, Layla pointed down the street and said, "is that it?"

"Yes. It is." He handed the cash to Layla. They got on board, and he told her to put four singles into the vending machine. She grabbed the pass that the machine dispensed, and they sat down together. They were halfway to the hospital when Layla's phone interrupted their conversation.

"Hey, what's up?" she answered the call.

Her phone was loud, so Dak could hear the guy on the other end ask what she was doing.

"Nothing, I'm just on the bus."

"The bus? Busses are filthy. People get stabbed on busses. Besides, my family's dinner is later on. Why are you out instead of getting ready? You won't be back in time."

"The hospital isn't that far, and we weren't going to be long at all. Just relax," said Layla.

"No. I'm sending Henry. Text me your location."

Dak began to think maybe he was right to assume what he had about Layla that first day of therapy. If she associated with people like that, then maybe she was just as spoiled as the rest of the people in North Torino. Then he thought about the time they'd spent together and hoped that she wasn't like the person on the other end of the phone call, but rather that she just didn't know of any other way. She did get on the bus, though, which people like that wouldn't have even considered.

Dak returned to reality when Layla said, "Sorry, Dak, I gotta go. Mitchell is sending a car to pick me up."

"It's getting dark out. Will you be okay?"

"I checked, and there is a Geralds restaurant near here. I can wait in the lobby until my ride shows."

"Just pull the string on the window, and the bus will stop for you." He watched as she stopped the bus and walked off.

"There goes my last four dollars," he thought.

Dak walked through the automatic doors and shoved his hands into the pockets of his jacket. He got into the elevator and pressed the button for the third floor without removing his hands from his pockets.

"How do you survive in this freezer?" he asked his father when he got into the room. "Even in the winter, it's warmer outside."

"I'm barely surviving. Besides, you don't know about winter, Dak. We're in Florida. There is no such thing," his father said, flipping through the channels on the television. He stopped when the weatherman came on tv. "See, it's sixty-five." He continued changing channels. "Back at home I-"

"Rode your bike to school in the snow. I know, dad."

"What bug crawled up your pants today, son?"

"It's nothing. Have you been watching tv all day?"

"What is this 'nothing?' Is it school?"

"No. It's just that..." Dak threw himself into the chair in the corner of his dad's room and looked up at the ceiling. "I was supposed to introduce you to my friend from therapy today, but something came up while we were on the way over."

"You made a friend through counseling already?" He put the remote down.

"Yeah. Her mom is sick too, so she kind of understands what I'm going through."

"Oh. Is her mom a patient here?"

"No. Her family has money. She gets treated at Torino General."

"Well, she must be a real nice girl for you to be this disappointed. What's her name?"

Dak sat up in his chair, looked at his dad, and said, "her name is Layla, but it's not like that."

"But why not," his dad teased.

"Because, dad, she has a boyfriend. That's why she couldn't come."

"That's fair enough. Well, what have you got for me today?"

Dak pulled a box out of his bag and stood up. He handed it to his dad while he wheeled over the side table. Dak placed the box on the table, opened it up to reveal a game of checkers, and sorted the chips that were inside.

As he moved the first piece, Mr. Reynolds asked, "so what happened with her boyfriend?"

"We were going to take the bus, and he sent a car to come to pick her up instead. Can you believe that?"

"What do you mean he 'sent a car' to get her?"

"I mean, we were on the bus, then he called her, and then she got off. I guess one of his butlers came to pick her up or something." The game had picked up, and Dak paused to consider his next move. "Apparently, they had dinner plans, though, so maybe he just felt like she was going to blow him off," Dak explained as he took one of his dad's pieces off of the board.

"Does she know you feel this way?"

"What do you mean? It doesn't really matter what I think. I don't even know the guy."

"I meant, does she know how you feel about her?"

"No," Dak stopped mid-move, "I don't feel any way about her. I told you we are just friends." He took another one of his dad's pieces off the board. "Anyways, I came here to win, not to complain."

"Well, you were telling me on the phone about mom's book. What's up with that?"

"Are you trying to distract me?"

"It doesn't matter. You're beating me anyway."

Of course, with the mention of the book, Dak brought up Layla again. Dak's dad attentively listened to his son. His conversations with Dak were the best part of his life for the past two years. Nothing that Dak had brought into his hospital room could have been more exciting than the idea that Dak would finish his mother's work.

"Where is your writing? I'd like to see what you've got so far."

"Um…" Dak collected the last of his father's pieces from the board. He turned around to pull papers from his backpack and handed them to his father. "These are the options for the cover design," he said.

"Wow. These are great, but you don't draw. Where did you get these?" Dak's dad asked as he shuffled through the illustrations.

"Layla made them. Which one do you like?"

"This one." His dad held out a sketch of a girl lying on the beach by a nest of turtle eggs. "Well, I am glad that you are working on your mom's story. I'm proud of you." He put the papers down on top of the open game of checkers and sighed. "I have something I gotta tell you, though. My doctor has been running some tests."

"Is it bad?"

"I haven't gotten the results back yet. I won't know for a couple more weeks."

"It will be fine, dad. They have been taking great care of you, and you've been looking better lately, too. Let's not worry about it until we get the results, okay?"

"Alright."

Dak went home that night, and he never felt more alone. He immediately tossed his bag on the floor, then threw himself on the couch while he checked his phone-no texts from Layla. Dak didn't want to bother her with something that might be no big deal, but she was the only person who understood his situation. "She's probably still with Mitchel anyway," he thought to himself.

Dak sat up. He looked at the clock on the stove and dropped his chin in his hands. It seemed like hours had passed as he got lost in his thoughts, but by the time he came back to reality, he realized it had only been seven minutes. Dak's clothes suddenly felt heavy, but he didn't have the energy to remove them. He rested the back of his head on the pillow and stared at the ceiling, imagining how content he was before his dad mentioned the test. He thought he was distressed before, but this worry exceeded any amount he had ever had.

He looked over to the mess he and Layla left in the living room. Dak's thoughts went to the moment his father asked about her. Maybe his dad had a point. Dak wondered why he was so disappointed that Layla hadn't come to meet his dad. Layla's computer was still on the side table, and as he looked at it, he realized he missed her. He didn't care so much about how she left as he did about the fact that she wasn't there.

Dak never had many friends, and he couldn't get very close to the people he knew. He was afraid of meeting new people in therapy, so he didn't think he would actually end up with a friend, let alone find someone like Layla. He walked over to the record player and put on the song they had listened to together the day he met her mother. Dak felt grateful for their friendship, but he was more confused now than ever.

His mind wandered back to the news his dad gave him, and he remembered that Layla's mom was dying too. "Ugh. Stop thinking about her!" They had spent so much time together lately that he hadn't thought anything about his feelings. Still, he considered them to be what anyone would feel when they finally found someone they can relate to.

Dak stared at his phone, wondering if he should say anything to her. After a while he gave in and texted Layla.

Dak: I don't know how to say this, but I kinda miss you.

Dak: Oh, and you left your laptop and some stuff here!

• Chapter Six •

As soon as Mitchell's driver dropped Layla off at home, she jumped in the shower.

Mitchells parents were nice. Well, Mr. Simmons was always nice. There was tension between Mrs. Simmons and Layla. Layla stayed in North Torino County just as the Simmons did, and she lived an extremely comfortable lifestyle. But Layla's mother didn't have nearly as much money as Mitchell's parents. Because of this difference, Mrs. Simmons always treated Layla as if she wasn't good enough for her son. Mitchell never helped as he tried to get Layla to see things from his mother's perspective.

Layla was very anxious about what to wear. There was no way for her to know what would impress Mitchell's mother, so she played it safe and wore a black dress.

Just as she had finished getting ready, she got a text from Mitchell letting her know he was outside. Layla looked at herself in the mirror one last time. She could see the pain she was holding as if it were trapped behind her eyes. She had tried to mask it with make-up, but she could see through it. Layla was exhausted from crying herself to sleep every night, yet waking up early to go to school. She stayed up late thinking about the invisible timer that was tracking her mother's death. She took a deep breath and promised herself that she would try to enjoy herself tonight.

Mitchells driver, Henry, stood outside of the car and held the door open for her. He gave her a compliment on her outfit and a positive affirmation as he always had.

When Layla sat inside the car, she noticed the partition was up between them and the driver. Immediately Mitchell demanded, "you know, I still can't believe you were riding the bus today. Who is this Dak guy?"

"He's someone from group therapy. I'm editing this story he's writing. He wants to submit to the Gold Pen Foundation, actually."

"As if the GP would accept someone like-" Mitchell could see Layla's face changing. "I mean, I wish you two the best with the story. Actually, Meredith Fowler should be in attendance tonight. She sits on the board. I could introduce you."

"That would be great." Layla smiled.

"There it is-that beautiful smile of yours." Mitchell said.

"Anyways, I was on the bus because I have to get my car fixed. I'm pretty sure it just needs a new battery."

"Do you need me to take care of it?" Mitchell asked. Layla wondered if Mitchell had ever taken care of anything himself or if he had always fixed his problems with money. If the battery were ever to die in his car, he likely would have Henry drive one of his father's cars instead. Granted, Layla could drive her mother's car if needed. Still, not even her mother's car was anything like what Mitchell arrived in.-

"No, Mitchell, I can handle it. I already had it towed to my mechanic. I should have it back tomorrow."

Once they arrived at the Veranda on the Oaks, Layla began to feel nervous. Mitchell told her to be herself and to show the room her beautiful smile. She agreed, but she didn't even know what he meant by that. Honestly, Layla didn't care about this event. There was a room full of people gathered for something that wasn't grief, and maybe for an hour or so, she could pretend that she belonged here. The place was beautiful and bright. The floor was made of marble that was so clean Layla could see everyone's reflection.

"Layla! I didn't expect to see you here. What a pleasant surprise," said Mr. Simmons.

"Yes, what a pleasant surprise it is," Mrs. Simmons said sarcastically.

"Good evening, Mr. and Mrs. Simmons."

"Layla, I have some people I want to introduce to you," Mitchell said. He wanted to keep Layla and his mother as far apart as possible.

Mr. Simmons interjected, "working the room, I see."

Mitchell snapped his finger at his father as he pulled Layla away. "Just like you taught me, dad."

Layla and Mitchell walked away from the group and toward the end of the ballroom. They sat at a tall table for two next to the terrace overlooking the garden wall.

"Let's sit here for a minute while I find Meredith, then I can introduce you." Mitchell surveyed the room. "I'm only doing this so you can succeed, by the way," he said smugly.

"I get it, but Dak is just a friend, so you should be glad you're doing something nice for other people too. Not just your girlfriend."

"I know, I know, I just want you to be successful. If this is how you are going to go about it, then that is fine. Get into books just like your mom. She was successful at it, and I bet you'll be great too. You just need a couple of doors opened for you." Mitchell looked back at Layla. "Over there, the lady who is just walking in. The one with the short gray haircut wearing a pantsuit."

"That's her? She looks nice," Layla made eye contact with Mitchell, "but that doesn't mean I'm not nervous."

"Don't be nervous. Come on." Mitchell took Layla's hand and ushered her over to Meredith.

"Meredith Fowler?"

"Yes?" she responded.

"I believe you're sitting on the board of the Gold Pen scholarship with my dad, Martin Simmons."

"Oh, so you must be Mitchell then. Your dad brags about you all the time," she laughed. "And who is this?"

"This is Layla. She is writing a book and entering it for a chance at the scholarship. I thought maybe you could give her a leg up." Mitchell winked. "She's been going through a hard time because, well," he lowered his voice, "her mother has cancer."

Layla looked at Mitchell from the corner of her eye.

"I'm sorry to hear that," Meredith said.

"It's been difficult for us, but I thought that if Layla could find somewhat of a mentor during this time, it could push her to accomplish her goals."

"What is this book about?" Meredith asked Layla.

"Actually, it's not just me. I am editing it for a friend. He is writing about a young marine biologist who is protecting sea turtles. It's terrific, actually," Layla said.

"Hm... I'd like to hear more about it. Here is my card. You can call me during business hours if you have any questions about the scholarship or need any assistance."

Layla was thrilled. She couldn't wait to tell Dak about this.

"And that's how it's done," Mitchell smirked as they walked away, but his facial expression quickly changed once he saw how angry Layla was. "What's the matter? I introduced you to Meredith," he said, "I thought you would be a little more excited."

"That's not the point, Mitchell! Why did you have to use my mother dying as if it's some sort of bargaining chip or divisive leverage for you to play around with? It was incredibly inconsiderate."

"I'm sorry. I wasn't trying to disrespect you or your mother, but if you can use it to your advantage, then why not? She's going to die regardless."

Layla was furious. She knew that Mitchell couldn't understand her because he wasn't losing a parent. Still, his lack of empathy towards her grief was intolerable.

"You know what Mitchell-"

Before she could finish, Mitchell took a glass off of a table and stood on a chair, tapping the glass with his long red acrylic nails in the process.

"Everyone, I would like to grab just a moment of your precious time. Would you please do me the honor in acknowledging the beautiful person that is my girlfriend, Layla Porter?" He reached for his jacket pocket. "It's not an engagement ring, but a promise ring to the girl I love so dearly."

He stepped down from the chair and placed the ring on Layla's finger as she faked a smile for the audience. As the magic wore off and the guests continued on with their own agendas, Mitchell asked Layla what she thought of the ring. Layla's fake smile disappeared, and her face turned back to its previous state of fury.

"You know what, Mitchell, fuck off!" She threw down the promise ring before running out of the venue.

"What am I going to do now," Layla pondered.

She didn't want to be at the party anymore, but she didn't have a way to get home. She started to walk down the Oaks' driveway when she remembered that she still had the all-day bus pass that Dak bought for her earlier. Layla looked inside her purse, and there it was: a literal ticket away from "Mitchell Fest featuring The Snobs." She looked up the nearest bus stop on her phone and found that it was actually not that far of a walk.

Layla pulled the strap of her purse across her chest. She started to walk toward the stop with her phone in one hand, and using the other hand, she clutched the pepper spray in her purse. Layla thought about how uncomfortable it would be to ride the bus alone.

"I'm sorry that I abandoned you earlier for my arrogant boyfriend, Dak. Still, I don't want to ride the bus alone, and you're the only person I know that actually rides the bus. Ugh, I can't actually say that," Layla thought to herself as she debated contacting Dak for assistance. She thought it might be a bad idea to say anything at all. The only other way for her to go home would be to call a taxi or something, but she didn't really know how to do that either. Layla started to walk back toward the venue in defeat when suddenly her phone buzzed.

Dak: I don't know how to say this, but I kinda miss you.

Dak: Oh, and you left your laptop
and some stuff here!

> **Layla:** So you're not mad at me?
> Because I don't want to ride the
> bus alone.

Dak immediately called Layla and asked her what was going on. She explained the fiasco she had with Mitchell. Dak suggested that he direct her through the phone to help her navigate the bus system, but she was worried that it was getting late, so she asked him to meet her.

"Where are you exactly?"

"I'm at the Veranda on the Oaks near downtown."

"Well, there is a transit center near my house. I can take bus six and be there in twenty or so minutes if I leave now, but you should get to the nearest stop soon. Take bus four and ride it to the transit. It should take you about thirty minutes if I remember correctly."

It was both terrifying and exhilarating for her to get on the bus. When she placed her ticket into the machine, it sucked it up and spat it back out. She didn't really know where to sit, so she asked the bus driver if she could sit in the front. The bus driver laughed and told her she could sit anywhere she wanted. During the bus ride, Layla had a lot to think about. She had never paid much attention, but the lights on buses never went out even at night.

Because of the bright white light colliding with the evening sky on the window, she could easily see her reflection. Who was the girl looking back at her? Who was she supposed to be, and how was she going to put the pieces back together? Her mother was dying, and her relationship was on the rocks. There was so much to think about, and the bus had not even reached its first stop.

Minutes had turned into hours and back into seconds, then the bus notified its patrons that the next stop was the transit station. As the bus approached, Layla prematurely pulled the string in excitement. She stood up while struggling to maintain balance in her heels. She was the first person off of the bus, but Dak wasn't waiting for her. Layla needed to keep moving, or she would be blocking the exit. There was a bench nearby, so she decided to sit there and call Dak. Layla nervously dialed his number while constantly shifting her head around. Before she could even get a dial tone, a voice spoke from behind her.

"I want two million credits for this." Layla immediately turned around to find Dak, who she trampled with a hug.

"I'm so glad to see you!" She took a deep breath, "thanks for coming."

"What can I say? I guess I just really missed you."

Layla grabbed Dak and told him that she felt terrible about leaving him earlier.

"It's okay, really."

"Listen, I know you can be recluse at times, which makes for not having a lot of people in your life, but you can't just say it's okay because you will be accepting less when you deserve much more. You're my grief buddy. I should have been there for you today like I said I would be, regardless of if you needed me there or not. That's not what friends are supposed to do." She grabbed Dak's hand, and they got on the bus that would take them back to Layla's house.

• Chapter Seven •

Weeks had passed, and Layla wasn't ready to go to group therapy without talking to her mother first. Most therapy days were fine, but she needed extra time with her mom because of the eulogy. She only had three hours between school and therapy, plus she still needed to pick up Dak, so she had to make the visit quick.

As Layla walked down the hospital halls, she caught glimpses of different people inside their rooms. Some were temporarily sick, and others terminally ill. Watching all of these people filled her with anger. She thought about how her mother would have to live out her final days in such a depressing environment. Layla stood in-front of the door of her mother's room and took a deep breath before she knocked.

"That's my lady. I know it," her mother said as Layla opened the door.

"Hey, mom." Layla smiled. "Hey, Darla," she said as she walked into the room. Her mother's best friend visited as frequently as Layla had.

"Hey, Layla, honey. I have been here a while. Let me give you two some time alone." Darla kissed Layla's mom on the forehead and hugged Layla before leaving.

"I know you're worried about me. I can see it all over your pretty face. Have you been sleeping well?"

Layla had all of these emotions, and she couldn't hold them inside any longer. She burst into tears. "I'm trying to be strong, but I feel like I can't hold it together. I just know that I'm going to end up alone with no one. I mean, you're all I have in this world, and now you're leaving me." Layla paused and thought about how her mother must feel. She immediately regretted putting these feelings on her mom's shoulders, but she also felt better letting it out.

"I'm so sorry you have to go through this, baby. If I could, I would walk out of here with you today," her mother said.

"I know. I just want to spend so much time together. That's why I have been coming here almost every day, and I brought nail polish this time."

"Is it the color you're wearing? It's hot."

"Yep, so we can match, and you haven't had a spa day in forever, so I thought this might help."

As Layla began to paint her mother's fingernails with the light blue color, Ms. Porter said, "you know, I'm so proud of you."

"Proud of me for what?" Layla didn't break her focus, but the look on her face was confused.

"You're such a strong young woman, and I know you can stand on your own two feet. You don't need me, or some boy or anyone to define you, lady. I know you're scared, but you will pull through this and come out of it all stronger. I love you, Layla."

Layla smiled. She had only painted two nails, and she was already crying. She expressed to her mother how much she loved her.

"I've been thinking a lot about it," Layla said as the tears subsided, "and in a way, this eulogy is my last chance to honor you. I just don't know how to translate that into a speech."

"You say whatever you need to. It doesn't have to be long or serious. Just say what's on your mind," Layla's mother responded. "Where did you get this nail polish, by the way?"

"I had to do some research because I know you will get irritated by the fumes, so I ordered this kind off of the internet. I tested it out on myself first, obviously, to make sure it's safe."

"Did you get any more colors?"

"Just this one, for now, to see how we like it." As Layla was speaking, she spilled some nail polish on her mother's skin. "Don't worry," Layla said. "I'll just let it dry. It will peel right off. Another perk that was listed on the nail polish website."

"How much was this magic nail polish?"

"Don't worry about that. Anyways, Dak actually helped me figure out a little bit of what exactly is 'on my mind,' like you were saying. I took him to the park, and he interviewed me, so I would have some ideas about what to write."

"That's nice of him to do. Maybe working on it with someone else will make it easier for you. What's up with this Dak boy, by the way? Is Mitchell out of the picture yet?"

"What do you mean 'yet'?" Layla paused her procedure to look at her mother.

"You know, Mitchell isn't- nothing. I just think Dak is nice, respectful, and down to earth."

"Well, he's only a friend. He just happens to be a good and helpful one." She continued painting. "Almost done."

"Alright. If that's all, he is." Layla's mother rolled her eyes.

"Nails are done, and in sixty seconds, they should all be dry."

Talking to her mother made Layla feel a lot better because they could always talk about so much in so little time. Before leaving, Layla gave her mother a kiss and told her she was glad to have her as a mom.

When Layla got to therapy, she felt like her head was slightly clearer about the eulogy. Still, she was more emotional about it than ever. Suddenly it seemed real.

"Sometimes dealing with my mother's illness is extremely lonely," Layla began the session.

"How so?" Jade asked.

"I guess it's because we've known our parents our whole lives, and we've all only met each other this year? Having this group is supportive, but it's just that I think I'm used to my mom always being there. I mean, at breakfast, at night, when I'm sad, all the time. Now not only am I having to pre-grieve without her, but it's about her!" Layla started sobbing. "My mother only has three months left, and I don't know what to do!"

"There is nothing wrong with not wanting to be alone, but there is gratification in finding your own independence. Take your mother's death as an opportunity instead of a burden," Jade said.

The group murmured in agreement. Some chimed in with experiences similar to Layla's to make her feel less alone.

"If it makes you feel any better, my mom passed away last week, so I definitely know what you are going through," another kid from the group chimed in.

"Thanks, and I'm sorry about that," Layla heavily sighed. "I'm sorry that I am being so selfish. At least my mom is still here, and I have a little time left with her. I should appreciate it." Layla stood up. "I think I just need to go home."

Before she reached the door, Jade said, "I would like you to stay, but it's okay if you are overwhelmed and need to take a break. Go value the time that you have left with your mother."

It was silent as she walked out of the room, and Dak looked around at everyone. "Um," he said after a moment, "she's my ride home, and I kinda want to make sure she's okay, so I'm going to go too..."

"That's alright, Dak. We'll see you guys next month."

Outside, Dak tried to catch up to Layla, who was running to her car. He stopped when he saw a guy get out of his car and start talking to Layla. Dak sat on the short brick wall outside of the building and waited out of sight, but after a while, it seemed like Layla's conversation was going to be long. Since therapy was going to be over soon, there was no use in returning. Dak got up and sulked to the bus stop.

Mitchell tapped on the window of Layla's driver's side. She wiped her tears and rolled down the window.

"Why are you here?" Layla asked.

"I came to surprise you. And look," Mitchell pulled coloring books from behind his back. "I brought you a gift." Layla took them and put them in the passenger's seat. She rested her head on the steering wheel and cried softly.

"What's wrong?" Mitchell asked.

"I feel so selfish because there are people whose parents are already dead, and I can't even enjoy the time I have left with my mom, and I should be allowed to be upset because my mom is dying, and I don't think I'll ever get over this, and-"

"Okay, okay, stop. These coloring books are supposed to help you relieve stress or something, so I thought I would bring them to you at therapy- ya know, where you relieve stress?"

"Coloring isn't going to stop my mom from dying!"

"Well, Layla, nothing can stop that. I can only help you deal with it."

"Then you can actually talk to me about how I feel, or ask me about my therapy, or you could be there for me, as in do more stuff together, like cooking with me! Or not canceling our date to go golfing!"

"Cooking? But you don't even cook…"

"Forget about it."

"Well, what else do you need," Mitchell asked. "Do you need gas money?"

"No. I gotta go."

"Okay. Well, um, about your mom's funeral… I… I can't make it."

"That is the last thing I needed right now, Mitchell! I told you I needed you there for me!" Layla proceeded to start her car and sped out of the parking lot.

Later that night Layla decided to text her mother.

> **Layla:** Are you tired? I don't feel very good, and I wanna talk to you about it.

Mom: What happened?

> **Layla:** I was flustered, so I left therapy early, then Mitchell and I

got into an argument. I am too
stressed to even process my day
because I am still concerned about
you and this living funeral.
I feel like you're giving up, and
writing a eulogy makes me feel
like I am letting you give up. It's
like I think it's okay or something,
and I'm just going along with it.

Mom: We talked about this
earlier, Lady. You're scared,
but you're strong enough to handle
 this. You will be able to
stand on your own.

Layla: I am too young for this!

Mom: This is why Darla suggested therapy, but I
understand it will take a while to come to terms with
everything.

Layla: Therapy has been helping,
but it's just not going to fix this.
Nothing can.

Mom: The only thing we can do
is be here for each other <3

> **Layla**: I am only going to write
> this eulogy to support you, but I
> still feel like writing it is like
> condoning that you've accepted
> defeat. Anyways, I guess I'll get to
> it.

Layla pulled out her notebook in which she kept all of her ideas and emotions. On her phone, she had the recording of her interview that Dak sent her. She went question by question and wrote bullet points that she thought might be good for the eulogy. After multiple breaks to eat, watch tv, and organize her closet, Layla was only halfway through the recording. It had just become too much.

She stared at the bullet points and felt a tightness in her chest. She tried the breathing exercise Jade and Sienna had them do in their sessions. Four counts breathing in. Hold for four counts. Four counts breathing out. Layla dropped the notebook on the floor and cried into her pillow. Layla picked up her phone and gave Dak a text.

Layla: Are you awake?

Dak: Yea

Layla: I need someone to talk to. I'm so anxious right now.

Dak: Can I borrow your car?

Layla: ???

Dak: You know, so I can take you out for ice cream, and we can talk about it.

Layla: Lol yes. I'll be right over.

When Layla got to Dak's house, he was waiting outside for her. He was just standing there with his backpack, but there was something that just seemed different about him.

"Oh! Your hair looks nice. It's so curly and fluffy," she said when he got into the car.

"Thanks. I uh... just washed it."

Layla got out of the driver's seat and sat in the passenger's side.

"What are you doing," Dak asked, laughing.

"You said you wanted to borrow my car to take me to get ice cream. So, here is my car, and here I am," she said as she shooed him to the driver's side of the car. Dak walked around the vehicle to the driver's side. "So, where are you taking me?"

"Well, it's incredibly late, and I'm incredibly broke, so I'm thinking Gerald's."

"Gerald's? a burger chain?"

"Yes! And, before you say it, I know their ice cream machines never work, but because of our parents, maybe the universe will throw us a bone."

"I hope you're right."

On the way to Gerald's, Dak told Layla that he saw her arguing in the parking lot with someone earlier.

"I don't want to get in your business, but I just care about you and want to make sure you're alright."

Layla smiled at him. "Well, Mitchell waited for me outside of therapy as a surprise, but it kind of backfired. He and I just haven't been able to work like we used to. It's almost like my situation has forced me to grow up a bit and be more independent. I guess the person who I am becoming isn't as compatible with him as I had hoped."

"Who is that person?"

"The kind of person that can stand on her own two feet even if she doesn't know what her next step is going be. Someone who finds comfort in people but isn't dependent on them."

"I think I like that Layla much more."

"Well, what does the next Dak Reynolds look like," Layla asked as they approached the drive-thru intercom.

"Hold that thought," Dak said as he rolled down the window. "Hi, can I get two ice cream cones?"

"I'm sorry, sir, the ice cream machine is broken."

Dak glanced over at Layla, who shrugged her shoulders. Dak had a backup plan. He thanked the cashier and pulled out of the Gerald's parking lot.

"Where to now?" Layla asked.

"I got a different plan; we're going to the drugstore."

"I mean, it's not soft serve, but I will take it."

Once they got to the drugstore, they grabbed two pints of ice cream. Layla got chocolate, and Dak got mint chip.

"I'm going to go grab some spoons. If you see anything else you want to snack on, it's on me... as long as it's under two dollars."

"Big ballin', I see. Ha, okay, I will take you up on that."

After they paid for their ice cream and snacks, they locked the car doors and sat in the parking lot. It was quiet for a second, and Dak started to feel nervous.

"I'm sorry for being so quiet," Dak said after a while.

"It's okay. I like sitting in silence. It's actually quite comforting."

"So, about your eulogy..."

"Nope, you're not getting off that easy. You still haven't answered my question."

"What question?"

"What does the next Dak Reynolds look like?"

Dak placed a big scoop of ice cream into his mouth and held up his finger.

Haha, funny, but I can wait. You will eventually run out of ice cream," Layla said, taking a bite out of her potato chips.

"More confident somehow," he said with his mouth full.

"Well, I think you're on the right path. It takes confidence to go for the GP scholarship."

Layla's words were reassuring. For such a long time, he lacked the confidence to follow through with his ideas, but he started to see that he was changing just like Layla. He had a friend, and he was actively pursuing something. For the first time, he felt like the person he always thought he could be.

"Can we play some music? I actually found this new song that's older than us both, but I know you will like it." Dak connected his phone to Layla's car and played an old R&B song. As the song played, they spoke about music and the band's history. As they talked, they also compared writing songs to writing books.

Dak turned down the radio as the next song came on. "We're pretty close to finishing this book, but we don't even have a name," he said.

"Do you have any ideas?"

"Not really."

"I mean, a book title should be subtle. What do you think?"

"We already have the cover design. Why don't we get some ideas from that?"

"Well, the cover you chose is the main character on the beach, making sure the sea turtles get out to sea."

"Yeah?"

"What if we call it something like Escape into the Moonlight," Layla suggested.

"Well, the turtles are Olive Ridley because those are my mom's favorite animal. She did a lot of research on them and fell in love. Maybe we can incorporate that."

"Olive Ridley Sea Turtles Escaping into the Moonlight is too long of a title, Dak."

"What are they escaping from? They are going into the moonlight."

"That was supposed to be a joke, but yes. They are Olives going into the moonlight."

"Olives in the Moonlight?" Dak suggested.

"Olives in the Moonlight. Yeah. Good." Layla grabbed the pint of ice cream from Dak and a spoon from the bag. "I was thinking about those baby sea turtles from the story the other day. In a way, you and I are no different."

"How so?" Dak asked.

"Well, I'm losing my mother, and you have already lost yours. We are both very young, and just like those sea turtles, I feel as though we are looking for some guidance and wanting to escape our situations and feel safe and realized."

"I never looked at it that way." Dak turned down the car radio. "I think you already know what you want to say during your mom's eulogy."

"Wait. what?" Layla said, confused.

"I just wonder if maybe your subconscious is keeping you from writing anything because it will make losing your mother seem more real."

"You know, you're the only person that seems to get me sometimes. Only you would say that. I think you're right."

"Don't give me too much credit. I have been in your shoes."

"Yeah, maybe I am holding myself up."

"I think you will be able to finish it."

Layla scraped the bottom of Dak's ice cream pint and asked him what he planned on doing after graduation in a couple of months. He told her that he just wanted to start Torino Community College and figure himself out before committing to some long trek. The truth was, Dak had been so caught up in his dad's illness and in losing his mother that he really hadn't thought about what he wanted.

Layla knew she wanted to go to art school, but she didn't think she was emotionally ready for a huge commitment. She was thinking about attending TCC as well. Layla hadn't told anyone, especially Mitchell, because she felt embarrassed that she couldn't handle a school with more prestige. But that was the old Layla, and the new Layla didn't care about those things at all.

• Chapter Eight •

It was a warm January evening. The kind of
winter night that only Florida is capable of producing.
The sky wasn't dark or grim. In fact, there was no rain or
a long funeral procession- just a large group of people
gathered in a luxurious venue. Everyone wore black, and
some were crying. The crying would stop and then start
again. Layla pictured the guests crying over her mother's
casket, but then she remembered her mom was present
in the building.

Family members came to speak to her one by one.
Most of these people felt like strangers. Her mother had
no siblings, so most of Layla's cousins, aunts, and uncles
were sort of distant.

Even though Mitchell had told her in advance that
he wouldn't be able to make the wake, it still hurt her.
She felt like Mitchell had abandoned her in her hour of
need. However, Dak was present and very anxious.

"Why are you so nervous?" Layla said to Dak as
she rubbed the lipstick from her tooth.

"I don't know. I just don't like funerals. I know
this isn't technically a funeral, but it still feels the same."

Layla closed her compact mirror. "Dak, I don't want to make you uncomfortable. You can go if it is bothering you that much. I promise I won't be upset."

"No. I want to be here for you. It's important to you, so it's important to me." Dak took one last sip of his water and asked Layla where the bathroom was.

"It's down that hall to the left."

As Dak walked away, Layla went to check on her mother in her dressing room. When she got near, Layla could hear a conversation between her mother and one of her mother's friends. The woman was asking her about a surgery that Ms. Porter was downplaying.

"What surgery, mom? What are you talking about?" Layla popped her head into the dressing room.

"I'm sorry, Denise," the woman said as she walked away.

"Mom, what were you talking about?" Layla looked at her mother's nurse, who was seated in the corner. "What surgery?"

"Layla, we don't need to talk about this now. Can this wait until later, lady?"

"It's a surgery that you're denying, isn't it? A surgery that can probably save your life! I knew it! You're giving up. I can't believe how selfish you are!" Layla ran into the bathroom that was in the dressing room and locked the door behind herself.

Dak left the men's bathroom and wandered around the venue looking for Layla. Eventually, he found her mother, who was upset. Layla's mom explained the situation and suggested that maybe he could go and talk to her. Dak felt that it would be best if the two sorted it out themselves, but Ms. Porter had exhausted herself from beating on the door. She excused her nurse so she and Dak could speak to Layla.

"Layla?" Dak knocked on the bathroom door.

"This is so fucked up!" She was sobbing hysterically.

He asked her to open the door so that they could talk, but Layla just wanted to be alone. Dak took off his thrifted suit jacket and rested it upon a nearby chair. He assured her that he wasn't going anywhere. Through tears and heavy breaths, Layla told Dak about the conversation she overheard. He looked at Ms. Porter, who shrugged and shook her head.

"I know you don't want to hear this, but death is just a part of life," Dak spoke up. After a pause, he continued. "The first experience will always be jarring, but I will be there for you. You can get through this."

The room was silent.

"Layla, baby, I just want you to know that I'm here for you. Please, can we just talk about this?"

Layla continued to cry while ignoring them both.

"I know we've already talked about this, and I'm not trying to make you feel ungrateful, but you really should enjoy the time you have left with your mom. Say goodbye to her while you can." Layla was still crying and didn't have the energy to respond. "My... um, mom. I didn't get the chance you have right now. I didn't get to say goodbye. She was walking through our old neighborhood, and she got hit by a stray bullet."

Ms. Porter closed her eyes and shook her head as a tear rolled down her cheek. All three sat in silence for a while until Layla finally came out and gave Dak a hug.

"I never knew. I'm so sorry. I just assumed that maybe she had been sick too." She exhaled and wiped her eyes with some tissue. "Thanks for sharing that. I'm sure it was hard for you to talk about."

"I just didn't want you to lose sight of the opportunity you have in your possession, Layla."

"I'm sorry, mom. I can't stop thinking about losing you. I just want to explode. You're the most important thing to me." Layla and her mother hugged for a moment before Ms. Porter signaled Dak for a group hug. Layla felt

so much love from them both that she felt compelled to deliver her eulogy.

"I'm ready to speak. I can do this."

"You know, lady, you don't have to give some speech if you don't want to. I know what's in your heart."

"No, mom, I need to do this for myself." Ms. Porter left to visit with her nurse and alert the guests that Layla was prepared to start her eulogy.

"I'm going to sit right in the front. You can look at me the entire time if need be," Dak offered.

"Just like the one hundred times we practiced in your living room," Layla said as they walked out into the dining room. Dak squeezed her hand and told her she was going to do great.

From the stage, Layla looked out into the dining room. It was beautiful. There were little cocktail tables scattered throughout with white lanterns, and fairy lights were wrapped around the floor. It was both picturesque and fluent in her mother's style. It was a celebration of a life-her mother's life. As she approached the microphone, Layla took a deep breath and pulled out her phone.

"I promise you that I won't keep you long, but to be honest, I can talk about my mother forever. She is not only my candle in the dark but the wind that flicks at the wick—both the wisdom and the challenge in my life. You know, someone very special to me asked how I would summarize my mother in one word. But you see, that's the problem. I can't summarize her with such ease. It's why writing this eulogy was the most challenging thing I have ever written. How do you summarize the life of such a beautiful human with such a limit on words? So I thought about that question: one word, day after day, and night after night. Then I finally realized the word isn't about anything more or less than a simple perception. Mom- that's who she was when I mouthed my first words, and mom is who she will be when I breathe my last breath. You are beautiful from every angle Denise Porter, but most importantly, you have given me the best mom anyone could ask for. Thank you." Everyone in the room began to clap.

Dak teared up a little, listening to Layla. He missed his mother so much. He felt so bad for Layla because he didn't want anyone else to go through what he had to experience. Dak gave Layla a thumbs up as she smiled at him.

As Layla walked off the stage, Darla held out her hand to help her down the steps.

"Thanks for coming to support my mom," Layla smiled as she gave Darla a hug.

"You know I am the executor of your mom's will, so you can call me if you need anything. I'm going to be here for you during all of this."

"Yeah, thanks. If I need anything, I'll let you know."

For the rest of the night, many people spoke about Layla's mother. Different writers and poets, and people from all walks of life had come together to celebrate her. It felt good to be surrounded by so much positivity, and her mother seemed happy. At the end of the wake, as everyone was leaving, Layla's mother told her that she had enjoyed herself and that she loved the eulogy. She wanted to take a selfie with her, which confused Layla because she had paid for a costly photographer to capture the entire night. But her mother told her she wanted something genuine. It would be the last time she and her daughter would be all dressed up and in make-up together. Layla and her mother took many selfies then continued the celebration until it was time for her mother to return to the hospital.

• Chapter Nine Part 1 •

Layla was in a slump since her mother's wake. She had gone to see her mother on Monday, but her visit was cut short due to her mother having complications. Ever since then, Layla hadn't really left her bedroom. She had also only gone to school once this week, and it was already Saturday.

After his absence at her mother's living wake, Mitchell and Layla had grown distant. It had been an entire week since they spoke to each other face to face. It was early in the morning, and as usual, Mitchell had been texting and calling her non-stop. The irony of his communication skills is that if he had made an ounce of effort to physically knock on her door, she would have spoken to him. But Mitchell wasn't the "visit to see how you're doing" kind of guy. He was the "send you teddy bears and fruit baskets" kind of person. Layla hadn't spoken to Dak as much either, but Dak had felt her pain before. He was feeling this pain right now. Dak was giving her space out of enlightenment, whereas Mitchell was distant due to willful ignorance.

Mitchell sent her a text and said he wanted to get breakfast. Layla was reluctant, but she was hungry and too depressed to even order anything. He had suggested that they go to You Breakfast- a new restaurant that was do it yourself cooking. Layla thought about when she mentioned to Mitchell that they should do more stuff together. He now wanted to cook together, so maybe he had listened to her complaints. It was tempting for her, but she didn't want to ride with Mitchell and Henry after what happened the night at the Oaks. She was much more comfortable driving her own car.

When Layla arrived at You Breakfast, she was both surprised and impressed. There were other patrons at the small restaurant. She had expected Mitchell to rent out the entire establishment. In a way, it just showed her that maybe things were starting to change a bit.

"I'm so glad you came! I'm relieved to see you. I've been so worried since our argument," Mitchell said as he grabbed a stool for Layla.

She looked down before she sat. "I see you were able to get out of bed to get your nails done. Looks like you got a haircut too. You must not have been that down about it."

"You know, you gotta get up and keep moving," he smiled at her. His grin faded when he saw her expression. "You look starved. And tired. Let's eat. I'm excited to cook."

"Excited to cook? Who are you?"

"I just did some self-reflecting, and I had a really great conversation with my dad."

"Alright." Layla was intrigued but not without suspicion. As their conversation continued, Mitchell was more engaged and a lot easier to talk to.

The waiter, or "instructor," came to their table. They were sitting at a converted chemistry lab table with a non-stick griddle surface. Layla and Mitchell decided to cook omelets. The waiter asked what toppings they wanted and how many eggs, then they left shortly to retrieve the ingredients. As they waited, Mitchell asked about the wake. Layla didn't feel like going into detail about it, so she told him a version that didn't involve her bathroom breakdown.

When the waiter reappeared, Layla and Mitchell began cooking by cracking eggs into one of several glass bowls placed on the table. Mitchell tried to show off by lifting his bowl off the table and accelerating his whisking. Unfortunately, the egg passed the tiny apron that was provided and landed all over his shirt.

"Crap!" he said as he took his wallet and phone out of his pocket. "I'll be right back."

Layla laughed and continued to mix her eggs. Mitchell hadn't turned off his notifications, and his phone was ringing nonstop. Her phone buzzed as well, so she put the eggs down and checked it. It was a message from Dak, who seemed overzealous about something. He said he wanted to meet up as soon as possible. She told him that she was on a date with Mitchell and would call as soon as she was home.

Even after she was finished talking to Dak, Mitchell's phone was still vibrating. At first, she didn't mind, but the buzzing was persistent. She valued others' privacy and was neither the jealous type nor the kind to go snooping. But, the numerous text messages and Mitchells "new" attitude made her suspicious. The most recent notifications were from Mr. Simmons. First, Mr. Simmons asked how their date was going. Then he stressed the importance of Mitchell rekindling his relationship with Layla so they could get on with purchasing Sparrow Publishing.

Mr. Simmons had his hands in a lot of different industries- publishing being one of them. He had invested in several small publishers, but Layla never thought much of it. He was just a wealthy business investor with a healthy portfolio. Her mother, however, was a founder and a majority stakeholder at Sparrow Publishing.

Mitchell hadn't changed at all. He had just been coached by his dad on how to land a prospect. She wasn't his girlfriend; she was a business asset- a rite of passage for Mitchell on his pilgrimage to the business elite class. She was so angry that she didn't even want to give Mitchell the benefit of making her scream. She grabbed her purse, cleaned her hands, and politely waited for him to get back from the bathroom.

"I was able to get most of the egg off. Why are you packed up?" Mitchell asked.

"I want to be clear when I say this," Layla made direct eye contact with him. "I will never sell my mother's shares to you or any of your father's partners. You and your family are pathetic for praying on my sick mother. You don't give a damn about my mother or the fact that she's sick. You're trash Mitchell Simmons, and we're over! I don't ever want to see you again."

Layla stormed out and got Dak on the phone before she pulled out of the parking lot.

• Chapter Nine Part 2 •

Watching Layla and her mother at the funeral made Dak realize that he needed to take his own advice. His dad's illness had been such a regular part of their lives that Dak often forgot that he could lose his dad at any minute. He needed to appreciate all the time they had left together. Dak had visited his dad three times this week already, and he was on his way again.

"Surprise. It's me," Dak said as he walked into his father's room.

"Oh no, a visitor? I wasn't expecting this at all. You have caught me completely off guard. At least let me put on some pants."

"Wait, you're not wearing pants?" Dak asked seriously.

"I'm wearing a gown, Dak."

"Right, right."

"You've seemed pretty upbeat this week. Is there something you're not telling me?"

"Not really. I mean, you know I went to Layla's mom's funeral, remember?"

"Yeah. That's not very upbeat."

"I know, but I've been thinking a bit more positively since then. Watching Layla with her mom made me realize that I have an opportunity with you that I didn't get with mom."

"It sounds like therapy has been helping you."

"I'm glad I've been going. I have a lot of emotions about mom still that I have to sort through, and I've been thinking about bringing it up in therapy."

"You went through a lot when mom passed, and I couldn't get you the help you should have had back then, but luckily this therapy came up, so why not get it all out while you can?"

"Yeah. I just don't know what to say yet. I don't know how to explain how difficult it is to be going through this right now. No matter how positive I try to be, I am always just so mad that this is happening to you, and I don't know how to get over that."

"Well, just stop worrying about me," his dad shrugged.

"What?"

"Yeah. You don't have to worry about me anymore. I'm not going to die."

"What?"

"I got my test results back this morning," Dak's father teared up, but he let out a laugh, "I'm going to be home soon."

"Seriously? You're okay?"

"Well, the cancer isn't completely gone, but it's partially in remission, and the doctor says it's possible for a complete remission soon. You've seen me. I've been looking better. Not a lot better, but when you are in my position, son, you can feel it, and I've been feeling a little bit better every week."

"Wow. I can't wait to tell Layla, and, well, I guess Sienna and Jade. I want to tell everyone, but I don't have anyone else to tell. That doesn't matter so much because I've got my dad back!"

"I'll be back home, but I'll still have to come back to the hospital often to run tests and get checkups."

"That is still much better. I'm just so excited. I have to go meet Layla right now so I can tell her the great news."

"I still want to meet this girl you're so excited about, but maybe we can wait until I'm home."

"Alright. We can do that. I'll come by tomorrow and tell you how it went at therapy." Dak hugged his father, but he really squeezed him this time. The image of the frail older man in Dak's head started to regain a bit of his youth back. As he was admiring his father, Dak's phone rang. "Oh. Layla is calling. Got to go."

Dak left the room and answered the phone in the hallway. He took the stairs to avoid getting disconnected in the elevator.

"Hello?"

"Dak. You wanted to meet up? I can come to get you now. The date is over, and Mitchell and I are over too. But I'll tell you all about that when I see you. Where are you?"

"I'm just leaving the hospital, but you sound upset. Are you sure you don't want to go home and relax?"

"No. I've been over it since he said he wasn't coming to my mother's wake. I can come to the hospital and finally meet your dad."

"Actually, he just told me he wanted to meet you, but another day."

"Alright. I'll just talk to you when I get to the hospital then."

The second Layla pulled into the parking lot, Dak sped over to her car and hopped into the passenger seat. They had an hour to talk before therapy, so they shared their news in the car.

"I know you and Mitchell broke up, and that is important, but I have exceptional news, and my story is probably much shorter," Dak began.

"Go ahead."

"Okay. You'll never guess. It's really great. Also, um, I think I want to talk about my mom in therapy."

"I think that would be a good start for you, but is that the news you wanted to tell me?"

"No. I have more news; I'm just nervous and really excited too. Okay, so. My news is that they are letting my dad come home. They ran tests, and his cancer is in remission."

"That is fantastic. Wow, remission is amazing news!" Layla began to tear up. "I'm so fucking happy for you. This is excellent news, Dak."

"Well, it's partial remission, but he is going to beat this. I just know it! I'm so happy right now, I could kiss you."

Layla looked up at Dak and said, "just do it then."

She caught him off guard. Dak hadn't acted on his growing feelings for Layla because she was in a relationship, and he had an immense amount of respect for her. But here he was alone with her, and she was actually asking him to kiss her. Even though he was extremely nervous, Dak put his hand behind her neck and gently pulled her closer. There was instant chemistry between the two of them. They had finally crossed over from being just friends, but Dak wasn't sure if Layla really felt the same way or if she was just getting lost in the moment.

Layla rested her nose on his as they stared at each other. "Was that all you had to tell me?"

"That was it."

"Alright. After therapy, we can celebrate your dad's remission and my breakup with my awful ex-boyfriend. You'll never believe what I found out."

"What did he do, other than not going to your mom's wake?"

"Oh, that was bad, but this is even worse. First of all, I did not snoop through his phone. I just checked his notifications while he was in the bathroom."

"That sounds a little like snooping, but okay."

"His phone wouldn't stop going off! Not the point. His dad texted him, and they were plotting to buy my mom's company!"

"I don't understand."

"Apparently, his dad has been pushing him to be with me so he could manipulate me into selling my mom's shares after she passes."

"Are you sure? How did you get all of that from a text message? What did Mitchell say? I know I usually stay out of it, but these are some strong accusations."

"His dad said that Mitchell needed to fix our relationship so they could, verbatim, 'get on with purchasing Sparrow Publishing,' and Mitchell didn't deny it."

"Are you okay?"

"I am outraged, I feel used, and I'll probably cry about it tonight, but right now, it just feels great to have him gone. I'm seriously glad I caught them."

"I'm sorry that happened, but it's kind of for the better. You and your mom aren't being taken advantage of anymore."

"Yeah. Having to deal with all of this at one time sucks, but I guess I'd rather deal with my mother's illness without Mitchell. You were there for me more than he was anyways."

"That's bittersweet, I suppose," Dak said.

"Oh, something else that's actually bittersweet," Layla pulled out Meredith's business card, "is this."

"Okay. Who is Meredith Fowler?"

"Mitchell introduced us. He used my mother's illness to gain her sympathy, and now I have her card. She sits on the board of the Gold Pen, so she could have helped us. Though, I don't know if I can trust any of Mitchell's connections."

"He manipulated this lady by using your mom's illness?"

"Yeah. I guess that's just how Mitchell and his father operate."

"Well, I don't know if I feel comfortable moving forward with that either."

"Alright. I haven't called her, and I suppose I won't." Layla checked the time. "Oh. We gotta go."

Once they got to counseling, they got out of the car, and without hesitation, Layla held Dak's hand. He thought that this might possibly be the best day of the year. It was the best day he had in a long time overall. Dak had enjoyed his time with Layla throughout their friendship. Yet, he didn't know how excited he would be to hold Layla's hand because he didn't expect this to happen. The new chapter he had with both Layla and his dad made walking into this counseling session different. Dak finally had good news. He had something to say that he could be genuinely happy about instead of feeling like he was trying to get through a hard time with a positive mindset.

When they walked in, Sienna pointed to their hands and said, "are we doing couples therapy today?"

Dak and Layla dropped their hands without breaking eye contact with Sienna. They silently sat in their seats.

"I'm just joking, guys," Sienna laughed, "so what else is new?"

"I have some great news and something else I would also like to discuss," Dak spoke up.

"Where would you like to start?"

"I would like to start with my dad. He is going to be coming home. He looks a bit better, but he says he feels great, and his tests say that he is ready to leave the hospital."

"That's great, Dak. How do you feel?"

"I feel fantastic about it. I was terrified for a long time, and I have kind of forgotten what it's like to have my dad home, but now we can get some stuff back to normal."

"What will that look like?"

"Well, first, I'm going to have to seriously clean the living room before my dad finds out I've been living on the couch. Then I guess we'll have to take it slow until he's really better, but we can finally start watching movies and listening to music together again- in comfort, I mean, rather than in a hospital room."

"And this is all very exciting," Sienna said. "How are you holding up, Layla?"

"I'm really excited for Dak. I am trying to stay positive, especially with this great news, but it's just kind of hard. I've been feeling like a downer with how much I think about my mom."

"How have those emotions been affecting you?"

"I'm insecure about it. I don't want to drag everyone's mood down. I want to be happy."

"It is healthy for you to feel negative emotions during this time. You will go through a lot of grief, and anger, and depression before you will get better, but that doesn't mean you can't or won't feel happy eventually."

"We've been stumbling a lot lately, but you'll get back up and walk again," Dak added.

"And you don't need a miracle to do it. You need to look at all of the good things in your life and attach yourself to those. You can still be upset about the things that hurt. However, when negative feelings start to overwhelm you, you can cry about it if you need to, but then do something calming that makes you happy."

"Thanks," Layla said as she looked at the ground.

"So, what's the other topic you wanted to talk about, Dak?"

"I wanted to talk about my mom."

"Okay, good."

"My mom died a couple of years ago, but I never got help for it. I kind of just dealt with it, but my dad and I didn't know what to do or how to feel. Now I think talking about my dad has helped me heal a little bit more from my mom's death too."

"How so?"

"I will never be able to say goodbye, and I don't know if I will ever feel okay about that. But I got to talk about some tough things in here, and it feels way better to really say what's on your mind. It helps that other people in the Colors of Grief are going through the same thing. No one at school could relate to me when I was dealing with my mom's death. I've always lived in some bad neighborhoods, but I was never really friends with the kids from there. Most of the kids from school didn't get it because they lived in the suburbs. It's just-" Dak took a breath. "Sorry, that was a lot."

"Take all the time you need, Dak. So, the kids at school didn't understand your upbringing. How did that affect how you dealt with your mom's death?"

"She was hit by a stray bullet. Some kids acted like this happens every day, so it's just a part of life. They thought I wasn't strong enough to live whatever kind of lifestyle they wanted, but I was never on the same path as them anyway. Other kids didn't want to hang around me because they associated me with the neighborhood and nothing else. After my mom's death, we could finally leave that place. We're not living somewhere much better, but it is an improvement."

"So, how do you feel about finding us? We all relate. We all have different backgrounds. Has that been helpful to you?"

"I feel welcome here."

"Thank you for sharing that, Dak. We can talk more about it in a moment. I know we briefly mentioned your mom, Layla. How is she doing?"

"Well, she had a wake, and I have been taking all the time I can with my mom since then. She is really doing the best she can, and I have to go see her soon, but I am nervous."

"What makes seeing her this time different?"

"I broke up with my boyfriend because he was using me to get to my mom's company. I don't think I want her to know that."

"I'm sorry to hear that. How do you think your mom would react if she did know the truth?"

"I think she would be angry, of course. Probably the angriest I've ever seen her, but I don't need her being upset over something like that right now. She would be more mad that something like this happened to me. It would hurt her as well, but I don't think she would let me see that."

"So, you don't want to tell her the truth because you don't want to hurt her?"

"Yes, but I don't know if I can keep it to myself. She has a right to know."

"Well, Layla, whatever you decide, she will still love you. Know that this was not your fault, and she will still be there for you. Again, I'm sorry that happened, but if you look at it positively, they failed at trying to use you. You still came out on top."

"Thanks, Sienna."

The three of them talked about Dak and Layla's moms for the rest of the hour. It was something that they both needed, and talking about their moms was another thing that brought them closer together. They left feeling like some of the weight had been lifted, although not all of it. Of course, they knew it would take some time, but talking about what had been on their minds gave them a sense of clarity. However, Layla still hadn't made up her mind about what to say to her mother.

• Chapter Ten •

A lot had happened in the week since Layla last saw her mother. There was so much to tell her, and Layla was always nervous before visiting the hospital. She had been having nightmares of the day she would visit her mother for the last time. Layla had to tell herself that this was not the day. When she arrived, the woman she saw was a frail depiction of how her mother once was. Seeing her in this broken-down condition made Layla feel angry, but she was reluctant to bring it up. Her mother had always taken pride in her appearance. She was as close to vain as you could possibly be without overdoing it. Layla didn't want to make her mother feel ashamed of her looks, so she kept it to herself.

"Do you remember when we went to that roadside carnival? You had to have been ten years old," Ms. Porter said as Layla walked through the door.

"Yeah. The food was horrible, most of the rides were broken, and they didn't even have candied apples."

"Oh. I remember you wouldn't stop hollering about those damn candied apples." The room was silent for a while. "You know, as bad as we thought that day was, I had a lot of fun, lady. I've just been sitting in this room thinking about memories like that. So many moments in life that we declare bad are absolutely a blessing."

Layla placed her purse down beside her mother. "Well, good or bad, they're our memories, and I will cherish them even when I'm old."

"Old? You'll always be my baby," her mother chuckled.

"I'm eighteen, mom."

"Trust me. I know, but you have your entire life ahead. You will be a great artist, of course. And, who knows, you might fall in love one day."

"Well, I'm not too sure about that. Mitchell and I broke up."

"Good. I never really liked him. What happened between you two? And more importantly, why didn't you call or text me, baby?"

Layla was tense. She felt embarrassed that she had allowed Mitchell and his family to manipulate her in such a manner. Her mother had always been a model of independence and feminine strength for her. Layla didn't know if she had it in her to admit the truth. She felt like lying was her only option, but she had never lied to her mother before. At the cost of her and her mother's pride, Layla decided to tell her mother what happened.

"I'm so stupid, mom, and I feel so ashamed." Layla sank onto the bed by her mother's legs.

"What happened, Layla! Did Mitchell hurt you, or did something else happen? What is going on?"

"I broke up with Mitchell because-" Layla hesitated. She covered her face and placed her head on her mother's lap. "Because he was using me. He and his family were trying to manipulate me into selling your shares in Sparrow after you died." Layla cried hysterically.

Ms. Porter was furious. While she lay there wilting away, her daughter was being taken advantage of. She knew that if she reacted too emotionally, it would just make Layla feel worse about herself.

"You have nothing to be ashamed of, lady. You are a moral person, and you always try to see the good in people, even if they're rotten like that Mitchell boy. Sometimes in life, we make mistakes, and we have to learn from them. The wounds you carry from your disappointment with this relationship will soon heal and form wisdom. But, I want you to promise me something." She grabbed Layla's hand. "Don't ever let this world spoil you, baby. Be sweet and be kind. Be the person you have always been. Bitterness is a hard sentence to carry."

"I promise. You just always know what to say."

"I know I do," her mother said with a smirk, "but wisdom only comes with age, experiences, and a bunch of mistakes."

"I know it's not reality, but I just keep thinking about how foolish I would have been if he successfully got me to sell."

Ms. Porter burst into laughter. "Gotten you to sell?"

Layla didn't understand. She hadn't really discussed her mother's financial situation or even thought much about the will until the Mitchell incident.

"Why are you laughing?" Layla asked.

"Lady, you're eighteen. I was never going to just hand over all of my assets. You will inherit all of my personal belongings and the house. However, any money, shares, or anything financial won't be disbursed to you until you're much older."

"So basically, Mitchell's plan wouldn't have worked anyway? He probably would have just shown his true colors once he found that out."

"Possibly. But he's old news, lady. It's good that you found out when you did instead of much later."

"Yeah, and I haven't even told you about kissing Dak yet."

"Kissing Dak? Now I like that boy. He was so sweet and caring during the wake, and he makes some mean mash potatoes."

"Mitchell was always trying to impress me with what he could do for me. But all he really wanted was a dependent. Dak has been pushing me to be more independent." Layla told her mother how Dak had been there for her in the last few months and how he made her feel safe.

"That's what I like to hear."

"Dak's dad is in remission, actually. I have been giving him a lot of rides, but Dak has helped me so much too, so I want to do more for him. I want to do something special as a thank you."

"Something special like what?" Her mother asked.

"Well, I thought that maybe I could let Dak use my car for the time being, and I could drive your car. I mean, he takes the bus everywhere, and I know traveling will be more stressful now that he will have to help his dad more." Layla didn't know what her mother would say. Layla was in the position to help him and his father immensely. Ms. Porter had always taught Layla that helping others should be a requirement of living. She was a very charitable woman who helped fund multiple fundraisers through Sparrow Publishing.

"Your heart is in the right place, but I don't like your idea."

"Well, I thought I would at least ask."

"How about you *give* Dak your old car instead. You won't need it anyway."

"What do you mean?"

"Well, I wanted to surprise you. But to be frank, I won't be here for very long, baby, and you will inherit my car anyway. How about you take it now?"

"But, mom, your car is like eighty thousand dollars."

"I know, but it is of no value to me now. Think of it as an early graduation gift. Your car isn't anything fancy, so let's upgrade it."

Layla couldn't believe it. She and her mother were well off, and they lived in an elegant house, but aside from that, her mother made sure that they led a modest lifestyle. They ate at regular restaurants and wore non-designer clothing. Layla was the only kid in her neighborhood that didn't have a driver or own a car worth more than nine thousand dollars. To the kids in her community, Layla's car was unacceptable. To Layla, it was a sign of trust from her mother and a gift of independence. Regardless, Dak would be much better off in her used car than taking the bus.

• Chapter Eleven •

It was now March, and Dak's dad was coming home in two weeks. Ms. Porter, on the other hand, had been getting worse. With every trip to the hospital, Layla could see her mother slowly deteriorating. Even though her mother's death was on the horizon, Layla's visits persisted. She had been going to Torino General every single day. At home, she kept her mind busy by preparing for the Gold Pen Scholarship submission. Dak and Layla had finally submitted a final draft of Olives in the Moonlight and was waiting to hear back from the program.

Dak and Layla were supposed to carpool to therapy as usual, but today was special. Layla suggested that Dak drive her car to therapy, and she would drive her mother's car. This way, they could go home separately so she could "take her mother's car to the mechanic" after therapy. Dak obliged, and they arrived at group therapy in separate vehicles.

"You're extra cheesy today. What are you up to?" Dak asked Layla as he closed her car door.

"I'm just so happy around you," Layla said.

Dak grabbed Layla's hand and said, "I know we aren't official, so I want to give you as much time as you need to process your last relationship. But if you didn't already know, you're everything I've always needed and all the beautiful things I never even knew existed." Dak kissed Layla on the forehead. Dak had always been a caring friend, but ever since they kissed, she had seen a more intimate side of him. They kissed again for a moment and then walked into therapy.

This week's session started as all sessions had. Jade asked everyone to summarize the way they were feeling at that exact moment. Not everyone always participated, but it was a good ice breaker. Eventually, it was Dak's turn to speak.

"I feel positive for once. My dad's cancer is finally in remission, so this nightmare is almost over."

"I feel so very happy for you, Dak. You know I gotta ask; how does that make you feel?" Jade followed up.

"Well, when I found out, I was ecstatic. My world stopped in a way. I felt like I was waking up from an early morning nightmare. But as I thought about my mom a bit more, it made me sad that she couldn't beat death the way my dad is. Even now, as I'm sitting here, I look around this room, and I see a bunch of people who, even in their misery and grief, are excited for me- somewhat of a stranger. It makes me feel supported."

Most of the group immediately chimed in, reassuring Dak that they were happy for him. Layla was going to wait until after therapy to gift Dak the car, but since the attention was already on him, she thought it would be the perfect time.

"I actually have an announcement for Dak," Layla suddenly spoke. The room got quiet, and everyone's eyes shifted toward her. "Well, I think that it's great that your dad will be getting out of the hospital soon. I know you don't have solid transportation, so I am giving you my car."

Everyone looked around the room. Some were excited for Dak, but Jade felt like Layla's approach wasn't proper during therapy. Everyone awaited Dak's reaction, but he was too embarrassed to say anything. Dak had already felt self-conscious around his therapy peers because many of them were from well off families. Layla had isolated him by emphasizing his need for transportation in-front of them. Dak's emotions ricocheted back at Layla sharply.

"I don't need any of your handouts. I guess I'm the loser here because I have to catch the bus, right?"

Layla knew this reaction was out of character. She immediately realized that she had embarrassed him, but it was too late. Her emotions had already spilled over.

"I was just trying to help! You're a being a jerk, Dak," Layla said as she stormed out of therapy, holding back tears.

Sienna followed Layla. Dak slammed back into his chair and kept his head down for the remainder of therapy. He just closed his eyes and listened, not really hearing anything that anyone had to say. Sienna eventually returned alone, which let Dak know that Layla had left.

After therapy wrapped up, Dak paced around the car. He contemplated giving the vehicle back to Layla and apologizing. He checked his phone to find a long message from Layla and figured he should let her have some space instead. When he looked up, a familiar face approached the car.

"You know, I really liked your book- well, most of it. Too bad your application didn't make it to the finals," Mitchell said.

"What are you talking about?" Dak asked, irritated.

"Nothing. I called a few people I know, and your little book isn't going to win. I can guarantee that. Where is Layla, by the way?"

"She's not here, and she told you to never speak to her again, so get lost."

"Well, that's too bad. Layla should be relieved, though. If I were her, I wouldn't want my name to be associated with such an amateur book. She should be thanking me," Mitchel said as he patted Dak on the shoulder.

Dak wasn't the violent type. However, Mitchell had not only insulted his book, but he also insulted the writing of Dak's mother, which infuriated him. Before Mitchell's hand left Dak's shoulder, Dak grabbed it, pulling Mitchell closer, and punched Mitchell straight in the face. The fight barely started before Jade separated them.

"Go drive away in your girlfriend's car, loser!" Mitchel yelled as he spit out the blood from his mouth.

"I want you off of my property now. And don't make me say that shit again," Jade said, making eye contact with Mitchell. Jade asked Dak if he was alright, but he rushed into his car.

"I know things are tough, but don't forget we have therapy Saturday!" Sienna shouted to Dak.

Sienna was right. Things were tough. As he drove home, he thought about how the evening had started in his favor, but everything had collapsed again. "Maybe this was the tuition for dad's remission," he thought to himself. Dak felt like he had grown so much, but tonight he proved to himself that there was still so much room for improvement.

• Chapter Twelve •

The seasons in Florida were always sprinkled with humidity and heat. However, there were cold days, and this day was noticeably chilly. Even the sun was wrapping itself in the clouds for warmth.

Dak had driven to Layla's house twice this week, but she didn't answer the phone or the door. He was angry with himself because of how he treated Layla in front of everyone. His dad was coming home soon, and he would have the privilege to drive him home himself. And it was for no other reason than Layla selflessly caring about him and his father's needs. He hadn't even gotten a chance to thank her.

It was the last Saturday of March. The doctors had given Ms. Porter until April to live, so Layla could lose her mother any day now. Dak felt even worse because Layla was isolated at such a time of need.

When Dak arrived to meet with Sienna at the Colors of Grief building, he was torn. He wondered if it was even worth it to walk inside, but Sienna was waiting, and he didn't want to waste any of her time.

"Hello, Dak," Sienna said warmly.

"Wow, you look like you're about to pop any day now," Dak said to break the ice. He was embarrassed that she had witnessed him lose his temper with Mitchell after last week's group therapy.

"Two weeks. The baby will be here in two weeks. But we're not here to talk about that. We're here to talk about you."

"I know. I still feel embarrassed about what happened at the last session."

"What do you have to be embarrassed about?"

"Well, Layla and I haven't really been talking, so I feel ashamed because I embarrassed her in front of everyone, including you."

"Let's first try to address your reasoning for the outburst. How does that sound?"

"Okay. I mean, I just felt uncomfortable because I am the only one in the group that doesn't have a car." Dak paused. "Well, I was the only one. I don't mean to sound offensive, but I didn't have another choice but to come here. My dad and I don't have the money to try anything else. Colors of Grief has helped me a lot, but I still feel a little bit like an outsider. Like maybe I'm being judged for being poor."

"So, how do you think those emotions caused the outburst?"

"I know all of the other kids are more well off than I am. So, when Layla made the announcement in front of everyone the way that she did, I kind of went into defense. Does that make sense?"

"Yes. I understand. So what do you have to be ashamed about then?"

"I felt ashamed about the situation I'm in, I guess. I try really hard, but I can't get to where other people are in life as easily. I just don't want any handouts."

"There is nothing wrong with how you are feeling. Have you considered that Layla may not have expected you to feel that way, and she was just trying to help?"

"I know she was just trying to help. I think I realize that now and I am happy that she-"

Sienna winced. "Sorry. I don't mean to interrupt."

"What's wrong," Dak asked.

"Nothing. It was just a little pain, something that just comes with pregnancy. Continue."

Dak tried to discuss his issue, but he got distracted when he looked down and saw that Sienna's water broke. "Oh, wow," he said.

Sienna looked down. "It's okay. Relax, Dak." She slowed her breathing. "Everything is going to be alright. I'm going to call Jade, okay?" She felt a sudden sharp pain,

"Oh! Never mind. This baby is coming now, Dak. This is incredibly unprofessional, but I need you to drive me to the hospital."

He nodded his head in agreement. Torino General was only eight minutes away. It was Saturday, so there shouldn't be much traffic, Dak thought to himself. He assisted Sienna into his car, and they made their way to the hospital.

Once they arrived, Dak helped Sienna into a wheelchair, and a nurse wheeled her toward the maternity ward.

"Thank you so much Dak, I'm sorry our session ended so abruptly," Sienna said painfully. One of the nurses assured Dak that she would contact Jade.

What just happened? Dak needed a moment to reflect. He decided that since he was already at Torino General, maybe he should pay Ms. Porter a visit. He hadn't seen her lately, and he wanted to thank her for the car.

Dak was surprised to see Darla and Layla outside of Ms. Porter's hospital room. Of course, he could have expected Layla to be there, but he hadn't seen her in what seemed like so long that looking at her instantly overwhelmed him. She sat on a bench in the hallway with her head in her hands. He approached nervously, and as he got closer, he realized she was crying.

"Layla?" Dak sat next to her and put his arm around her shoulders.

"What are you doing here?" She asked.

"Sienna is delivering her baby. We were in our session when she went into labor."

"Oh."

"What's wrong?" Layla started to cry so loudly that Dak could see passers-by attempting not to stare. Dak rubbed her back and waited for her to calm down. "Well, I came to thank you and your mom for the car." Layla didn't look up. "Um, is your mom okay?"

"No!" Layla looked up and wiped her nose on her sleeve.

Darla interjected, "Denise passed away, Dak."

"She's been drugged up all week, and now she's gone! The last time I get to see her, and she's a freaking zombie. I can't believe this. That isn't what she looks like. That's not even my mother!" Layla flailed her arms as she yelled. When she was finished, Dak hugged her and let her cry.

"Layla, sweetie, If you want to stay longer, we can- as long as you need. But we have been here all day. You should probably get home. Okay?"

"I'll be fine, Darla. You have already done so much. Go home and get some rest, please," Layla spoke gently.

Darla turned to Dak. "Will you stay with her? I don't think she should be alone."

"Yes. Of course."

Darla told Layla that if she needed her for anything to call her straight away. Darla had already prepared her guest bedroom just in case Layla wanted to stay over. Before leaving, she asked Dak to drive Layla home as she had come in Darla's car.

The two stayed at the hospital for a couple more hours. When Layla was ready to leave her mother, they drove back to Layla's house. The car ride was silent. There were so many things he wanted to say to her, but now wasn't the time. Layla was exhausted and just wanted to get some sleep.

When she arrived home, it felt different. This was a space she had shared with her mother for years. Her mother would never again walk through those doors. The house smelled like her, and it even looked like her to Layla. All of this was too much for her to handle.

"I don't think I can stay here tonight," Layla told Dak.

"I understand. It feels like your mom is occupying all of your senses. You can smell her, even taste the food she made."

"Yeah, and it hurts so much."

"Well, why don't you grab a few things, and I can take you to Darla's?"

"I didn't have to describe what I was feeling just now to you. I know Darla loves me and has my best interest, but she's never really lost anyone. I just thought that maybe I could stay at your place tonight?"

"Uh...yeah, sure. I think we can work something out. But please let Darla know. I don't want her to worry about you." Layla packed a bag, and they drove back to Dak's home for the night.

Dak had finally begun sleeping in his room again but decided to sleep on the couch tonight to allow Layla some space. At first, walking up the stairs into his bedroom felt weird. They had always worked and hung out downstairs whenever she came over. But there was this mystery about what his room looked like, and this was the moment she would find out.

"It's not much, but it's cozy," Dak said as he opened his room door. Layla was welcomed by a near spotless environment. There were color-coordinated records and some posters of her favorite bands. Tucked in the corner at the foot of a twin bed was a small writing desk that sat a little teddy bear.

"Who is this?" Layla smiled as she picked up the bear. Dak walked toward her, embarrassed.

"Oh, that's Pepperbear."

"Pepperbear?" Layla laughed.

"I couldn't say Papa bear when I was younger, so I kept calling him Pepperbear."

Layla smiled at Dak. "Thank you," she said as she gave him a kiss on the cheek." It was the first time she had smiled all day. Even if it was at Dak's expense, it felt good to share a laugh with someone.

"Well, it's kinda cold outside, so I'm going to go turn on the heater. Make yourself comfortable," Dak said awkwardly

"Okay." Layla put down her bag and removed the comforter from the bed. It was thin. The blanket sat cold all day, as did the home. The tears on Layla's face had dried, and she could feel the boundaries of their trails. She was too cold to bother wiping them off.

"It's still going to be cold for a minute, but I have a solution," Dak said as he reappeared. He asked Layla if he could have the blanket from her.

"Hurry up. I'm freezing."

Dak left and returned with a hot blanket and threw it over Layla's head.

"What did you do?" she said as she pulled the covers from over her hair.

"A little life hack: you take the blanket and throw it in the dryer on high heat and voilà."

"Genius," Layla said.
"More like broke. My mother would do this when I was little since we didn't have any heat on chilly days." There was a silence in the room. "Well, I will be downstairs if you need anything or if you want to talk."

"Yeah, I think I will try and get some rest." Layla tried to sleep, but she couldn't stop crying. Eventually, she exhausted herself and dozed off.

Dak, on the other hand, still wanted to apologize to Layla about everything that had happened. He never got to finish speaking to Sienna about his feelings. Through counseling, they had learned that writing about emotions was a great way to distract the mind while also getting things out of your head. He grabbed a pencil and began to write his mother a letter. Maybe talking to her would help him figure out what to say to Layla. Dak stayed up all night writing and typing away. Eventually, he also nodded off to sleep.

Dak awoke to the sounds of paper unwrapping and the smell of eggs.

"Layla? What are you doing?" Dak asked with one eye open.

She was at the kitchen table with a large bag from Gerald's.

"You must have stayed up a lot longer than I did. Since you were still asleep, I thought I would make us some breakfast. I don't cook, so I figured why not Gerald's."

"Thanks! I'm actually really hungry. Let me go brush my teeth."

Layla chuckled. "Dak, don't front. It's okay, you can eat first like a normal human. I won't judge. I promise."

"I'm so glad you said that because I'm starving."

Dak and Layla ate their food and talked about how bad Gerald's breakfast sandwiches were, and Layla shared some stories about her mother, and so did Dak.

"You are incredibly strong. I would be upstairs crying right now, but you're down here, and you went and got breakfast."

"I'm angry and so mad, Dak. I feel like it's not fair that my mother got taken from me when I already didn't have a dad. I think grief counseling is helping me a lot, though, because I am equipped to deal with certain emotions already."

"Well, it's like Jade always says it's okay to cry. We're supposed to cry. It's natural. But I actually have something to share with you." Dak wiped his hands on a napkin and walked to the coffee table to grab the letter he had written. "I wrote my mother a letter last night. I need to tell you something, and I just couldn't find the words. So, I wrote to her as an exercise to get it out."

"Someone was paying attention in counseling. Okay, so what do you have to say?"

Dak cleared his throat. "Dear Mom, I haven't spoken to you in what feels like forever. I don't feel like you ever left, because I think about you every day. Dad is better, and he is coming home soon. I have been so stressed out since you left, and then dad getting sick made everything worse. But, through all of that, I discovered and learned more about myself than I had before. I went to therapy, and I finally made a friend. She is beautiful and so selfless. She gave me her car, so I could bring dad home myself. Layla is strong and independent and even inspired me to finish your story. I recently let pride get in my way, and I embarrassed her in front of many people. I want to tell her how I was embarrassed because I am poor and felt like a charity case in-front of everyone. After giving it some thought, I realized that she already knew I was poor when she decided to become my friend. She knew I had dyslexia when she decided to help me finish the story. She knew I was a broken person when she decided to help me pick up the pieces even though she was broken. I just want to tell her that I am sorry and that I am more than honored to be in her life. P.S. Ma, I love you and miss you." Dak stopped reading and wiped a tear from his cheek.

"I don't know what to say," Layla said, teary-eyed. They hugged each other for a couple of minutes and finished their breakfast.

Dak told Layla about the fight he gotten into with Mitchell and how Jade had to break it up. Dak explained how Mitchell had called in a favor to get their book annexed from the Gold Pen consideration.

"Meredith Fowler! That must be who he has in his pocket. I totally forgot," Layla Exclaimed.

Dak didn't want to submit the story to a board that was so crooked. Layla agreed, but she still felt like they could do something about it.

"I have an idea," she sighed. "It requires that I call Mitchell, but I think it will work." Layla planned to record Mitchell and get him to confess about ruining their chances with the Gold Pen. All she needed was for him to name the individuals who had helped him, and it would be enough to go to the press and the board. Layla grabbed her phone and called Mitchell. She placed him on speaker and pressed record as the phone dialed.

"I was wondering when you were going to come to your senses. I hear an echo. Am I on speaker?" Mitchell said.

"My hands aren't free, and I'm not near my headphones. Dak told me about the Gold Pen situation. I have given it some thought, and I will consider selling the shares if maybe you can get Meredith Fowler to ensure that Dak's book is chosen for the scholarship." Layla bit at her fingers nervously and shrugged at Dak. There was silence for a moment.

"If we are going to move through with this, you can't inform Meredith Fowler about it. I just introduced the two of you because she was the only one in attendance at the Veranda dinner. Daniel Ofeeva and Lisa Jackson are the board members I got to remove your book. I don't even know if we could pull this off. It may be too late. I'll tell you what. I will give them a ring and talk to my dad, and I'll see what we can do."

"That's great. I will be in touch."

"Layla, I hope there are no hard feelings. It was just business. But I can see that you understand what that means."

"Yeah, no hard feelings. I'm all about business now. I have been enlightened," Layla said as she rolled her eyes in disgust. Mitchell and Layla said goodbye and hung up the phone. Dak suggested that they inform Meredith since she wasn't involved.

They spent the rest of Sunday writing emails and sending the audio to both local and industry journalists. They specifically targeted publications that were relevant to Mitchell's father's businesses. They made sure to email Meredith Fowler to give her a heads up about what they had done. Mitchell thought he had won, but soon Dak and Layla would expose him and his father for the cold-hearted crooks they were.

• Chapter Thirteen •

Layla had been dealing with depression in the last month since her mother's passing. Some days she was able to go to school and act like an average teenager, but today was not one of those days. Her mother was cremated, and Layla was given her ashes. Darla was going to Layla's house after school so they could drive together to some financial office to discuss Ms. Porter's will. The problem was that it was three in the afternoon, and Layla had just woken up. She hadn't showered in days. Someone was knocking on the door, but Layla was not in the mood to answer, so she placed the covers over her head and pretended not to hear them. The knocking eventually stopped, but her phone began to vibrate. It was Darla.

"Hello," Layla said nervously.

"Layla, I know you are at home. Let me in the door and stop playing games."

"Okay." She hung up the phone and drug herself to open the front door.

"Oh! Sweetie, you look a mess," Darla said once she got a glance at Layla's physical appearance. "And I know you have been dropping in and out of school. I talked to your guidance counselor."

"Darla, I'm depressed. Weren't you there? My mother is gone, and she's not fucking coming back."

"You can't just drop everything in your life. You have to fight through this."

"I know. I go to grief counseling, remember?"

"Yeah, and I spoke to your counselor Jade. She told me you missed your last session."

"Look, I know you care about me and want to look out for me, but I have this ball of confusion that is my life right now under control."

"Oh, really, and what exactly does that mean?"

"I'm eighteen, and I worked incredibly hard in school up to this point. That means that one, I cannot be in truancy, and, two, I have a pretty bulletproof GPA. I will graduate next month just fine."

"Layla, get dressed. We have things to do. I will be waiting in the car."

"Okay, just give me a minute," Layla said as she walked away.

"And take a quick shower, please," Darla yelled before closing the front door behind herself.

Layla hopped in the shower. When she got out, she stood at the sink and stared at herself in the mirror.

She smiled quickly, then her face returned to its depressive state. Layla heard Darla yelling her name from the kitchen and got dressed as fast as she could.

"I'm coming. I just got out of the shower."

"Did you see this?" Darla asked as she showed Layla an article on her phone.

"Is this real?" The article discussed the conversation with Mitchell that Layla had recorded. The Gold Pen Foundation was under investigation, as was Mr. Simmons and everyone who sat on the board. Dak and Layla's names were mentioned, but the article stated that there was no response to the inquiries.

"I haven't been checking my email either," Layla said as she pulled out her phone. Sure enough, there were tons of emails asking for interviews and more information about what she had sent out.

"They interviewed someone at Gold Pen, and they mentioned a book by you and Dak?"

"They did?" Layla continued to read.

"I didn't know you wrote. Let me read it. I can easily pull some strings at Sparrow."

"That would be amazing."

"Why didn't you just ask? I said if you ever needed anything," Darla said with her hand on Layla's shoulder.

"I don't know. I kind of wanted to do this on my own, but some help would be nice right now. I gotta tell Dak about all of this. I can't believe it!" This article getting out finally gave Layla a little sense of positivity.

"Tell him in therapy tomorrow. We have to go!"

Layla was nervous to read her mother's will. The older gentlemen named Ronald, who sat in front of them, was accompanied by two assistants. The name outside read "Franklin Hugh," and the building was enormous. There had to be at least five thousand employees working for this place.

Ronald began to speak. "I, Denise Porter, residing at 56 Crescent Way, Torino, Florida, declare this to be my will, and I revoke any and all wills and codicils I previously made.

To my partner and best friend Darla, I leave the task and honor of looking out for my 'Lady,' my daughter, Layla Porter. I leave all of my wine stock, including the aged ports, to her as well. There is a vintage blueberry mini dress from 1964. You always loved that dress, and I want you to have it.

To my daughter Layla Porter, I give all my tangible personal properties and all policies and proceeds of insurance covering such properties. This includes but is not limited to my sixty percent stake in Sparrow Publishing.

Any and all monies should be immediately transferred into the trust that has already been set up in your regard."

Layla raised her hand. "I'm sorry, but I never spoke about finances with my mother. How much did she actually leave me?"

Ronald looked at one of his assistants briefly. "Well, young lady, after expenses and taxes, your trust should be worth about twenty-two million dollars."

Darla chimed in. "Now, you will get a monthly expense of about four thousand dollars, but you will have to pay bills and be an adult. When you turn twenty-three, all the assets, real estate, and shares will be turned over to you, and the trust will dissolve."

Ronald kept reading until he got to the end. Layla already knew her mother wanted her ashes spread at the beach, and the rest was mostly arbitrary legal things. But once he was finished, he handed Layla a white envelope with a daisy drawn on the front. Layla knew the flower from anywhere because it was her flower. She drew the flower when she was eight and told her mother she wanted to be an artist. Inside the envelope was a letter her mother had written to her.

"Dear Lady, I know you are hurting right now, and I can only imagine how your skin must look from the stress." Layla began to laugh and cry. "I got you to laugh, didn't I? See, I still got it. I love you with all of my heart Layla. I know you are surprised at the amount of money I left you and the responsibility I have given you, but with it, you will be the mature, responsible and independent woman that you always have been. Since you have been going to grief counseling, I took it upon myself to do some research, and I want you to write to me whenever you want to. I know it sounds silly and, yes, I read it on the internet, but maybe it will help you, baby. I have tried to be proactive, so I left you a few letters for when you graduate and get married.
Xoxo MamaBear"

Layla wiped the tears from her face as one of the assistants retrieved a box from underneath the table. It was full of letters, each with instructions and descriptions on the envelopes. There was even a back-up flash drive on which Ronald's assistants had scanned a copy of each letter. Layla couldn't believe it. Her mother must have spent all of her downtime in the hospital writing the letters. There were dozens. Until now, Layla had felt alone, but she felt like her mother had left apart of herself with her after receiving the letters. This was the first decent day she had since her mother had passed.

On the way out of the building, Layla asked Darla how her mother owned so much of Sparrow if she was one of three founders. Darla explained that she owned thirty percent, and her mother had bought out the other owner completely. Now more than ever, Layla was interested in the inner workings of Sparrow. Darla told her there were so many stories to tell, so they went to dinner that night, and Layla learned more about her mother's legacy.

• Chapter Fourteen •

The next day Dak and Layla met up early at
therapy. Usually, they met Sienna on Saturdays, but since
she already started her maternity leave they didn't get to
have a final session together. She scheduled to meet
them on Tuesday instead. Layla had skipped group
therapy twice but was eager to meet with Sienna after
reading her mother's will.

Layla pulled up next to Dak in the parking lot, and
he got into her car.

"You look good. Have you been eating and getting
out of bed?" Dak asked.

"No. But I still can't believe this whole Mitchell
thing spun out into an entire investigation."

"Did you read the article I sent you last night?"

"I haven't gotten a chance to."

"Well, basically the entire board except Meredith
Fowler was into some shady business deals with Mr.
Simmons. Essentially there were already some folks
investigating them, but our audio leak was the spark they
needed to go public."

"Darla told me that my mother never told her
about Mr. Simmons trying to buy the company. I guess
she didn't really see it as a threat. Darla reiterated to me

that the company can't be sold for a while anyway because the majority shares are locked up in my trust." They talked more for another half hour before it was time to see Sienna.

Sienna was tired. She looked like she was at war with her newborn, and the newborn was winning.

"Not to be rude, but why are we meeting today? Didn't you just have a baby? Aren't you tired?" Dak asked Sienna when he noticed the darkness under her eyes.

"Jade has been doing everything for me here and at home. I really needed to get out of the house. Nonetheless, I wanted to meet with you both to properly end our counseling. You are both eighteen now and have progressed tremendously with handling the emotions associated with your parent's illnesses. I am happy to say that I am not worried that this is our last session together."

"Well, Dak and I want to thank you for all that you have done and the guidance you have provided us." Layla looked at Dak and smiled.

"Yeah, we were very disruptive and confused about our emotions when we first got to group therapy. Instead of kicking us out, you made this alternative therapy to accommodate our needs. It's been more helpful than you can imagine."

"Well, I actually learned a few things from this little experiment of ours. In combination with group therapy, I think the private sessions will be something that Jade and I will integrate into our next cycles of therapy. So, in a way, thank you for allowing me this experience as a professional."

"That's pretty cool. I think it will help a lot of kids," Layla said.

"Alright. I want to start off by asking the two of you two questions: What have you learned from group therapy, and what have you learned from our sessions?"

Layla went first. "Group made me realize that personal growth is the silver lining to losing someone. Here, I learned that my codependency was a crutch I needed to overcome."

"Group taught me about helpful writing techniques. You allowed me to be more open about my emotions so I could finally grieve my mother's death," Dak said.

"I'm really proud of you, the both of you," Sienna said.

After the session ended, Dak walked Layla back to her car.

"So, I brought my dad back home yesterday. You want to come over and meet him?" Dak asked.

"Are you sure? Is he feeling up to it?"

"Yeah. He told me he wanted to meet you soon, so I figure now is as good of a time as ever."

"Is he feeling better," Layla insisted.

"Layla, I was with you plenty of times while your mom felt like shit. My dad wants to meet you now. Come on."

"Alright, alright," she said as she got into her car.

When they got to Dak's house, Layla was surprised that the dining room had been transformed to accommodate a dinner of her favorite foods, including Dak's mashed potatoes.

"What's all of this for?" Layla asked.

"I just wanted to sit down and get to know you. My son talks an awful lot about you," Mr. Reynolds said.

"Really, like what," Layla said while smiling at Dak.

"Oh. She's direct, Dak. Straight to the point. Well, if you must know, I'm told that you have become a driving force in his growth."

"Dad!" Dak said, embarrassed.

"Is that right?" Layla said.

Mr. Reynolds picked up the dish of stuffing and passed it to Layla, "Now I know you like Dak's stuffing, but this is mine- the original recipe." Mr. Reynolds paused and exhaled. "Layla, I know you lost your mother to the battle. I want to personally thank you for all that you have done for my son. You gave him a shoulder to lean on and pulled him through all of this."

"I don't know what to say."

Mr. Reynolds laughed. "You can tell me how that stuffing tastes. How about that?"

The three ate and laughed. Dak's father had a joke for everything. He turned out to be a very positive and humbled man. After dinner, Dak's father embarrassed him by showing off his baby photos. When the night was over, Dak walked Layla outside to her car.

"So, did you give me your car because I was racking up too many points or what?" Dak joked.

She laughed. "No, that doesn't make any sen-"

Dak kissed Layla before she could finish her sentence. As they separated from each other, Layla noticed that Dak was holding a necklace in his hand.

"What's this?"

"Here," he said as he snapped the golden necklace around her neck. "It was my mother's; my father gave it to her when they started dating."

"Oh, so we're dating now?" Layla laughed. "Seriously, Dak. This necklace must mean a lot to you."

"You mean a lot to me," he smiled back at her.

Layla and Dak talked for a little while longer. When they were finished, he gave her a kiss on the cheek, and she drove home. It was the start of a new relationship for both of them. An adjustment for Dak and his father. The beginning of a journey for Layla. She was making a slow but effective process of coming to terms with her mother's passing. What her mother had really left her with was a challenge. A challenge to be independent and to stand on her own two feet. But most importantly, the will to be Layla Porter and to settle for nothing else.

END

If you have made it this far, we just want to say thanks for reading our story. Please feel free to visit our website for more updates and links to our social media if you're going to keep up with us. We look forward to interacting with you and delivering more stories for you in the future!

-B.B. & Dominique Keith

www.snailfingers.com